THE CHICKEN NUGGET AMBUSH

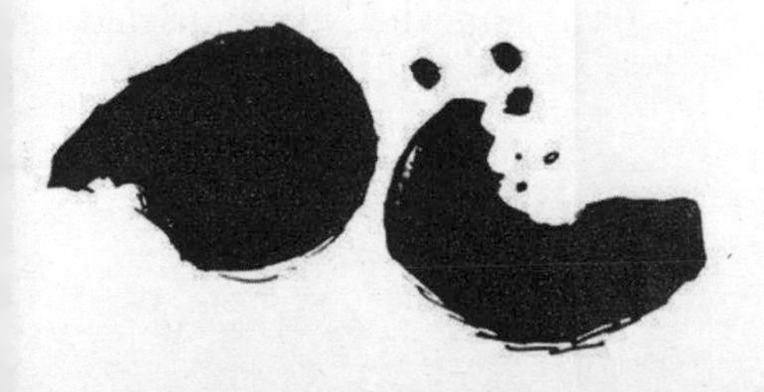

BY MARK LOWERY

The Roman Garstang Disasters
The Jam Doughnut that Ruined My Life
The Chicken Nugget Ambush

and

Socks Are Not Enough
Pants Are Everything

The Chicken Nugget Ambush

MARK LOWERY

Piccadilly
PRESS

First published in Great Britain in 2016
by Piccadilly Press
80–81 Wimpole Street, London
www.piccadillypress.co.uk

A CIP catalogue record for this book is
available from the British Library.

ISBN: 978-1-84812-484-4
3 5 7 9 10 8 6 4 2

Typeset in Sabon by Palimpsest Book Production Ltd,
Falkirk, Stirlingshire
Printed in the UK by Clays Ltd, St Ives plc

Piccadilly Press is an imprint of Bonnier Zaffre,
a Bonnier Publishing Company
www.bonnierpublishing.co.uk

For my lady wife and our three sproglets

You can't trust a chicken nugget.

Oh sure, they *look* harmless; boring even. Every single one is the same – a small, friendly-looking lump of chicken wrapped up in a crusty jacket. No surprises. Simple. Bland. Dull.

Only they're not.

They're nasty little critters. And like all cowards, they're only tough when there's a gang of them. They might seem innocent enough on the plate next to your chips and baked beans but, believe me, they're evil. While you're tucking into your dinner they're lying in wait, like little ninjas in bread-crumbs. And when you least expect it – *KAPOW!* – that's when they attack.

I should know.

I've never really liked chicken nuggets. They taste of cardboard and look like tiny deep-fried human ears, don't they? They're always either limp and squidgy or burnt and rock-hard. And if you buy cheap ones, the meat is kind of pale grey – exactly the same colour as the underpants you see hanging on an old person's washing line. Not to my taste.

Then again, I'm not really into any savoury food at all. Mum says I'm quite a fussy eater but I prefer to say 'careful'. I'll nibble bacon butties. Pies are OK. Sometimes I'll even force down a burger or a bit of cheese. But I don't *enjoy* these things. For me, eating savoury food is just something tedious you have to do so you're allowed a jam doughnut for dessert. It's like going to the zoo: eventually you get to see the exciting animals like the tigers and the penguins, but only after you've walked past the pigeons and the cockroaches and all the other rubbish ones.

This doesn't mean I've ever had any reason to be afraid of chicken nuggets, though. Not until recently, that is, when we went on our Year Six residential trip.

You see, I didn't know that chicken nuggets are completely vicious until it was too late. I wasn't prepared for the mayhem they caused and I just wish that someone had warned me beforehand.

So I think it's important that you read this story. It's all about how I, Roman Garstang, was ambushed by chicken nuggets.

Don't see this as just a book. See it as a survival guide.

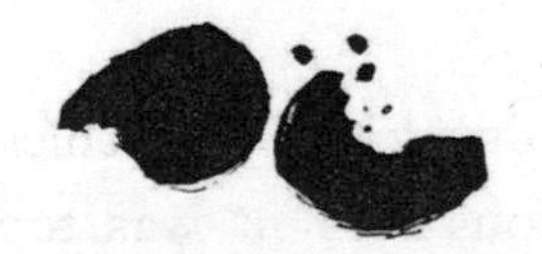

An Absolutely Awful Thing

Like I said, I didn't choose to eat chicken nuggets. They crept into my life and onto my plate like the sneaky little cowards they are.

For most of the last eleven years, I've enjoyed a diet that was at least fifty per cent jam doughnuts. I love them – their sweet stickiness, the crispy, crunchy layer of sugar on the outside, that thick pool of jam when your teeth sink inside. They're probably the greatest thing ever invented by mankind and I used to eat them all the time.

Up until recently, that is, when an Absolutely Awful Thing happened.

I'll explain . . .

I tried to eat a jam doughnut the other week and ended up being stung by a jelly-fish, covering my girlfriend in wee, shaving a guinea pig, getting banned from a super-market and being kidnapped by robbers (it's a long story)

↓

After all that, there was a tea party at our school for some old people, where the jam doughnuts caused the pensioners to start a riot (an even longer story)

↓

Meanwhile this horrible girl called Rosie Taylor was trying to shred some jam dough-nuts in order to get me into trouble (that one's a really long story)

↓

Unfortunately for her (but not for me), she knocked herself out after tripping over my best friend Darren Gamble's trousers. While she was unconscious a guinea pig gave birth on her face. Yes, seriously. This was so disgusting that . . .

↓

A kid in my class called Kevin Harrison threw up all over her (by the way, he's always throwing up, which is why his nick-name used to be 'The Vomcano'. Since he spewed on Rosie, people have also started calling him 'The Pukelear Missile')

None of these events was the Absolutely Awful Thing, though.

On the following Monday, Rosie's mum stormed into school and said that Rosie was too upset to come to class. And it was all the fault of me and my doughnuts. Apparently I'd intentionally turned Gamble's trousers, a pregnant guinea pig and the contents of Kevin's stomach against her! OK, so Rosie did have to spend two hours at the hairdresser having lumps of sick combed out of her hair, but now she was refusing to EVER come back to school unless Mr Noblet (our headteacher) **banned doughnuts**. **Forever**.

So he did.

Just like that. Without a second thought! Talk about unfair. Until then I'd always thought Mr Noblet was a nice man. Clearly I was wrong.

I was so devastated about the doughnut ban that *I* didn't want to come to school any more either. I mean, what exactly is the point of school if you can't eat a doughnut at break time?

Nobody cared about me, though.

In fact, Mum said, 'Well, if you're getting that cross about doughnuts, maybe it's time you stopped eating them altogether.'

Jeez. Thanks, Mum. What are you going to take away next? My legs?

So I wasn't allowed a single doughnut all week. Because of this my hands kept shaking and I didn't sleep properly for four days. I felt terrible, and when I did fall asleep I had nightmares about vampire doughnuts trying to suck the jam out of my veins.

Mum was worried I wouldn't be well enough to go on our residential trip so she took me to see the doctor. I was hoping that the doctor would tell Mum that banning me from eating doughnuts was completely mental and could easily kill me.

Unfortunately, she didn't.

In fact, the doctor said I was obviously 'addicted to doughnuts' so it'd be best if I **never ate one ever again.** Apparently I was 'suffering from withdrawal symptoms' and I'd be fine once my body got used to not having them any more.

Honestly!

How did that crazy woman ever qualify as a doctor?! That's like saying, 'Just stop breathing and you'll feel great in a couple of weeks.' How could I possibly be fine *and* not have doughnuts any more?

'Well, what *can* I feed him?' asked Mum, anxiously.

The doctor stood up to show us that the appointment was over. 'Oh . . . er . . . anything without sugar in it. Salads and vegetables, perhaps?'

'Definitely not!' I cried. 'I'd die!'

The doctor shrugged. 'If he's fussy, maybe stick to the same thing every meal. Now, what do kids like to eat? Hmm . . . I don't know . . . chicken nuggets, perhaps?'

Before I could demand a second opinion, she'd ushered us out and closed the door.

Chicken nuggets.

Little did I know that those two innocent little words would plunge my life towards absolute catastrophe.

The Nuggets Take Over

Sadly Mum took the doctor's advice way too seriously.

I mean, anyone could see that the doctor had just said the first thing that came into her head. 'Chicken nuggets' was just a *suggestion* of what I should eat. She'd only said it so we'd get out and stop wasting her time. She could just as easily have told Mum to feed me boiled cats or roasted tambourines or deep-fried ironing boards.

My mum is a real worrier, though. She treated the suggestion like it was a prescription of life-saving medicine! We sped straight from the doctor's to the supermarket (even though I'd been banned from there a few weeks ago). Inside, she rushed me right past the Squidgy Splodge Doughnut counter to the frozen aisle and filled the trolley with bag after bag of chicken nuggets.

After that I ate them **three times a day** for four days: nuggets and chips, nuggets and mash, nugget sandwiches, nugget curry, nuggets on toast. The worst meal was when Mum experimented with liquidised nugget porridge for breakfast . . . I know she was just trying to look after me but this was nuts.

By the time Monday morning came around, my burps tasted of old nuggets, my sweat smelled like old nuggets and I was pretty certain that my skin was forming a crust of crispy breadcrumbs. It's no wonder I was looking forward to my Year Six residential trip so much.

We were going to the Farm View Outdoor Survival Centre to learn how to live in the wild. But that wasn't what I was excited about. No – I was excited about having a few days away from home when I'd finally get to eat something other than flipping chicken nuggets.

This was a mistake. I should've been better prepared for what was in store. I should've been terrified.

MONDAY

Morning

When I Had to Survive a Full Moon and a Flooded Shoe

When Mum and I arrived at the school playground on Monday morning, most of my class were standing excitedly in groups with their suitcases. Their parents were all off to one side, chatting amongst themselves.

'Find your friends,' said Mum, 'and I'll just go and have a word with Mr Noblet.'

This didn't sound good. And anyway, what did she mean by friend<u>s</u>? I only have one – Darren Gamble – and he's a complete loony. On the other side of the playground, I could see Darren playing football with someone's suitcase so I decided not to go over.

I'd only been on my own for a few seconds when Rosie Taylor strode up to me. 'Why are you looking so sad?' she asked. 'Have you just realised you look like a turtle's bum?'

How lovely.

She was dressed like a mini-celebrity in a sparkly dress and high heels. Also, over the weekend her skin had turned bright orange, like . . . well . . . an *orange*.

'Yeah. I've had a spray tan,' she said, noticing that I was staring. 'Status update – get over it.'

A spray tan? She looked like a can of Fanta.

At that moment, Kevin 'The Pukelear Missile' Harrison walked past. 'Hi, Rosie. Nice tan. You look great,' he said, cheerily. Kevin's been super nice to Rosie ever since he sicked up on her.

Rosie didn't even bother to look at him. 'I've told you to stay away from me, Up-chuck.'

'But . . . ' began Kevin.

'Seriously, you grimalicious weirdo,' said Rosie, her forehead creasing in an angry frown. 'If you puke on me again it'll be a police matter. Hashtag – keep your distance.'

Shoulders slumped, Kevin scuttled off. I felt a bit sorry for him – he was only trying to be friendly. Then again, what did he expect? Since returning to school Rosie had been back to her awful worst.

After checking herself in a make-up mirror, Rosie put on an enormous pair of sunglasses. Then she pulled out her phone and began filming herself. 'Hi, YouTube fans,' she cooed, running her hand through her hair. 'Just one more ickle vlog post before I go on my Y-6 res.'

Why couldn't she just say Year Six residential?

She pouted at the camera. 'I'm gonna miss you guys *and* my pet pug, Cheryl. It's gonna be totes tough-icult. I mean, I've got to hang out with freasers like this . . . ' She turned the phone towards me for a moment then back to herself. 'Wish me luck. Mwah.'

'*Freaser*?' I asked, as she tapped her screen to upload the video.

'It's a mixture between a freak and a loser,' she cackled, clicking her fingers in front of my face.

Thanks a bunch. Then again, what else would you expect? Rosie's the worst person in the world.

One time she told everyone that I'd been born without a bottom and had to have one transplanted from a goat.

Rosie leaned right in to me and lowered her voice. 'Oh and *JSYK* – just so you know – I am going to *destroy* you at Farm View.'

'But why?' I exclaimed. 'You already got doughnuts banned from school!'

Rosie pouted. 'Er . . . because I've not forgiven you for everything you've done to me and I completely hate you, of course,' she said, then swept off across the playground. 'O-M-G. Everyone. Check out my new spray tan – the colour's called Midnight Walnut!'

As I watched her go, there was a sudden thump in my back.

'Ow,' I howled, turning around.

'Looking forward to Farm View?' grinned Darren Gamble, waving his fist at me. 'Everyone's on about the zip wire and the quad bikes but I just can't wait to go to the loo outdoors.'

I opened my mouth but there was nothing I could possibly say in reply.

Gamble is my best friend. Well, in the same way that a wart on my thumb would be my best friend

– i.e. stuck to me and impossible to get rid of without freezing him off or blasting him with a laser. When you only have one friend, you really can't afford to be picky.

He's small and skinny with a little shaved head that looks like a peanut, and he's always doing strange stuff. The other day we had show and tell in class. He brought in a jam jar. Inside it was a worm that he'd found hanging out of the back end of his pet dog, Scratchy.

Utterly gross.

It looked like a piece of hyperactive spaghetti. When he opened the jar and asked if anyone wanted to hold it, Kevin 'Pukelear Missile' Harrison had to run out of the room to throw up.

I'm not trying to be horrible by the way. Gamble's not evil or anything. Sometimes he can even be nice. And in any case, Kevin Harrison is *always* throwing up, hence his nicknames (as well as 'The Vomcano', he's also been known as 'The Chunderstorm', 'The Earl of Hurl' and, my favourite, 'Spewbacca').

No – Gamble's not a *bad* person. He's just naturally naughty and very weird. Hanging round with him is like eating fruit – perfectly fine now and again but you wouldn't want to do it every day.

'Where's your luggage?' I asked.

He held up a supermarket carrier bag. 'Gambles always travel light.'

I peered inside. Most of the bag was taken up by one of those giant plastic cup-and-a-straw things, filled with about a litre of luminous blue fizzy drink. Also I could see what looked like . . .

'A pen-knife, Darren? Really?'

Gamble isn't allowed near sharp things in school. There was an incident last month involving a knitting needle and some Year One kids in a game that he called 'human kebab'. Luckily his one-to-one teaching assistant Miss Clegg caught him before anyone was badly injured.

Darren put his finger to his lips. 'Sssshhh. Survival centre, innit. We might need to skin a squirrel for our tea.'

I rolled my eyes. 'What else have you got in there? A bear trap? An elephant gun? A nuclear submarine?'

Gamble grinned and opened his bag again. Apart from the blue drink, the only things I could see were a cheese sandwich (unwrapped), a flannel, a small torch and a book entitled *1001 Amazing and Disgusting Facts for Kids*.

That was it.

'Haven't you got any spare clothes?' I asked.

Gamble shook his head.

'Or underpants?'

'Eh?' he said, totally confused. 'We're only going for four days.'

I let this sink in for a few moments. 'That's quite a long time without changing your pants.'

'Nah,' he said. 'I'll turn 'em inside out tomorrow then back to front on Wednesday. And if they really stink on Thursday . . . I'll just go commando. Nothing like swinging free!'

I shuddered.

You might be surprised that Gamble was bringing a book. It was because he'd been told weeks ago that he needed to improve his behaviour to be allowed on the trip. He was so desperate to go that he'd even started reading and doing schoolwork. Amazingly, he hadn't got into trouble once in five whole school days.

Our teacher Mrs McDonald said that this was a record for him. Come to think of it, five whole *minutes* without Darren being told off was pretty astonishing.

Despite his best efforts, I wasn't sure if Gamble's behaviour *had* improved that much, though. On Tuesday he'd stapled a Year Two kid to a display board and on Wednesday he'd tried to inflate the caretaker's cat with a footpump. And I don't know who else could have written 'Miss Clegg is a hairy bumflake' on the boys' toilet wall. He didn't get caught for these things, though, so I don't know if they count.

Maybe he was just getting better at not being found out.

'Oh, and I forgot,' he said, dropping his voice and looking over both shoulders. 'There's something hidden at the bottom of my bag. I've got you a special treat for tonight.'

My eyes opened like dinner plates. 'You mean . . .'

My doughnut-starved brain went into overdrive. I imagined a Squidgy Splodge Raspberry Jam Doughnut. Round. Fat. Sprinkled with sticky sugar that glistened in the morning sun. Ruby-red jam oozing out of the hole at the side.

It was like I'd just crossed the desert and found water.

I felt myself reaching out for it and heard myself whispering, 'Come to me, my beautiful doughnut.'

Suddenly Rosie Taylor screamed: 'MR NOBLET! QUICK! ROMAN SAID "DOUGHNUT"!'

I snapped back into the real world.

How Could You?

Mr Noblet strolled over with Mum in tow. He was wearing sandals and socks, and a pair of far-too-small shorts. His legs were all white and hairy, like a pair of albino caterpillars.

Rosie was tugging on his sleeve with one hand and pointing at me with the other. 'He said it. Everyone heard him. You have to ban him from coming on the residential!'

'Bit extreme,' I protested. 'I only *said* doughnut. I didn't actually bring one.'

Rosie folded her arms. 'He's lying. Search his bag, Mr Noblet. Rosie Taylor is not getting on that coach if she has to share it with a jam doughnut.'

Mr Noblet stroked his moustache. 'If Roman says he hasn't got a doughnut then I –'

'The sewer rat must have one then,' Rosie

interrupted, pointing a bright pink false fingernail at Gamble.

'Oi, shut it!' said Gamble, wiping his nose with his shirt. 'I never said nothing about a doughnut and I ain't got one.'

I felt my stomach drop. 'What, really?' I muttered out of the corner of my mouth.

'Yeah. Really,' he replied, looking annoyed that I'd even asked. 'Why would I have one? They're banned and I'm a good boy, me.'

I decided not to mention the pen-knife in his bag. If he hadn't got a doughnut then exactly what kind of a treat had Darren brought me? Actually, it was probably better not to know.

'I know you're still upset about . . . *what happened*,' said Mr Noblet, patting Rosie on the shoulder, 'but I've just been speaking to Roman's mum. She's already phoned Farm View about his special diet. He won't be eating anything but chicken nuggets the whole time we're away.'

Rosie smiled cruelly. 'Fingers crossed they're poisoned ones.'

'How could you?' I blurted at Mum.

'Because I love you,' she replied, embarrassingly loudly.

Love?! Was she kidding? This was child cruelty.

Rosie narrowed her eyes. 'Well, you can't let those two sit together on the bus.'

'Darren will be next to Miss Clegg,' said Mr Noblet wearily.

'Huh. Three hours stuck with him,' yawned Miss Clegg, who was sitting on her suitcase a few metres away.

Miss Clegg is meant to spend all her time with Gamble but she can't stand him. I once overheard her say that 'working with that little maggot is like gargling with broken glass'. It was a pretty harsh comment, but I could sort of see her point.

I don't want to be cruel but Miss Clegg looks a little bit like the Honey Monster and she always appears to be half asleep. To me she looks and sounds permanently depressed. Her voice is sad and pathetic, like an early-morning trump when you're still half asleep.

'It'll be alright, miss,' grinned Gamble, as people started making their way to the coach. 'We can listen to music on your phone. Have you got "Badger Massacre" by The Scuzzy Toilets?'

'No,' sighed Miss Clegg. Darren has very weird taste in music – really loud heavy metal that sounds like an explosion at a drum factory.

'How about "Cactus Underpants" by Doctor Torture and The Lethal Injections?'

'Of course not.'

'"Diarrhoea Grandad" by The Scabby Sparrows?'

Huffing out her cheeks, Miss Clegg forced herself to her feet and shuffled towards the coach. 'I hate my life,' she mumbled under her breath.

A Surge of Awesomeness

There was a bit of a scrum around the luggage hatch of the coach. This was mainly caused by Rosie Taylor, who'd brought three massive leopard-print cases with her. 'If anything gets broken,' she warned the driver, 'I'll sue you so hard that your children grow up homeless.'

Mr Noblet shouted over the top of the noise that we needed to keep our packed lunches out for when we stopped. After dragging my case over to the driver, I tucked my miserable box of cold chicken nuggets under my arm and trudged to the steps. On the way past, Mum gave me a horrible slobbery kiss. 'Oh, Roman. What will I do without you?' she wailed, suddenly all tearful and snotty.

Now you know how I feel about the doughnuts, I thought, as I extracted myself from her suffocating hug and climbed up the stairs onto the coach.

Mum wasn't the only person in the playground who was crying. All the other parents were blubbing away, as were the kids who weren't coming on the trip (including my ex-girlfriend Jane Dixon, whose parents are way too protective to let her go away for two nights). The only person who wasn't crying was our teacher, Mrs McDonald, who couldn't come because she didn't want to leave her new baby guinea pigs overnight. In fact, she looked totally delighted to be waving us off for three days.

I didn't want to look at Mum's tear-stained face as we drove off so I sat on the far side of the coach and gazed out of the window. Three rows ahead, Gamble was violently rocking Kevin 'Pukelear Missile' Harrison's seat and shrieking, 'Come on, Kev – let's see the multi-coloured fountain!' while Miss Clegg played with her phone and half-heartedly told him to stop. Far behind me, Rosie Taylor was telling everyone to get off the back seat because it was reserved for 'the queen of the bus'.

I was glad to be on my own.

For about thirty seconds, anyway.

'Alright, Roman?' said a chirpy girl's voice behind me. 'Mind if I sit here?'

Before I could reply, Vanya Goyal had already plonked herself down in the seat next to me. I tried to say something but I couldn't.

Vanya Goyal is pretty much the coolest girl in our class. I suppose she's a tomboy and a little bit of a rebel. She's amazing at football, she goes to Scouts, she plays the electric guitar *and* she's a black belt in karate. Her hair is thick and wild like a lion's mane, and she's got a tiny little nose stud (even though they're against school rules). She's mega popular with everyone because she's always cheerful and bouncy but I've never really got to know her too well.

The engine of the coach coughed into life.

'Saw you on your own and thought you looked lonely,' she said, giving me a friendly dig in the arm.

I struggled to think of something to say. When your only friend is Darren Gamble, you tend to be nervous around normal people.

'Plus there was nowhere else to sit,' she laughed. I smiled weakly.

The coach started to move forwards and everyone cheered.

Vanya clapped her hands together excitedly. 'This trip is gonna rock!'

I shrugged.

Her face dropped a bit. 'Hey. Come on. I don't wanna sit next to a mute. What's up?'

'Nuggets,' I said, showing her my lunchbox.

Her reaction took me by surprise.

'No way!' she said, her huge brown eyes opening wide. 'Nuggets for lunch? My favourite. You're so lucky!'

'Really?' I replied. 'I can't stand them. They were forced on me by my mum and an evil doctor.'

'Tell me about it,' Vanya sighed. 'I've only got a wrap and a crummy doughnut.'

My jaw dropped open. 'A . . . what?'

'A wrap. Tuna and cucu–'

'No, no. The other thing,' I said, suddenly aware that I was panting like a dog in a sauna.

'Oh, the *doughnut*,' she said, like it was no big deal – when clearly it was the biggest deal ever. 'I don't even like 'em. It's Dad. He got the letter about the doughnut ban last week and said he'll feed me what he likes. He doesn't like being told what to do, see? He says you should always stick it to the man, whatever that means. I've taken one to school every day since but I usually put 'em in the bin.'

Putting doughnuts in the bin? That's like flushing beautiful paintings down the loo. I made a sound like a hungry baby owl. Luckily Vanya didn't seem to notice.

'It's like when Mr Noblet said I couldn't have my nose pierced but Dad just . . . ' Her voice trailed away. 'Er . . . Roman. Are you OK? You're kind of . . . drooling.'

'You've really got . . . a DOUGHNUT?' I cried, grabbing her by the shoulder.

Vanya frowned and smiled at the same time as she peeled my fingers off her. 'Er . . . yeah. And?'

I gulped. 'When you've finished it, can I . . . lick the bottom of your lunchbox?'

Vanya gave me a funny look. Straight away I realised how weird this sounded. What an idiot! What would I ask next – *can I pick the bits of half-chewed dough out of your teeth? Can I scrape the jam off your chin?*

There were several seconds of awkward silence. Then Vanya burst out laughing. 'Ah, Roman. I never realised you were so funny!'

Phew! Go with it. She didn't realise I was being serious.

'I've got a better idea. I'll swap you my wrap and doughnut for your chicken nuggets,' she said, offering me her hand. 'Deal?'

'Deal,' I replied, an incredible surge of awesomeness sweeping over me. I felt like I'd just swapped a go-kart for a Ferrari. 'Shall we do it now?'

'Do what now?' said Mr Noblet, sleepily turning round to face us. He was sitting across the aisle and one row in front.

'Nothing, sir,' said Vanya innocently. When he'd turned back round, she flashed me a mischievous smile, her nose stud winking in the sun. 'Reckon you can wait til we get there?'

Maybe, just maybe, this trip wouldn't be so bad after all.

Black Belt

The journey to Farm View took almost three hours but I hardly noticed. Once I knew that I'd soon be munching my favourite snack, my mood improved by a billion per cent. Vanya and I chatted and joked the whole way there.

We played Twenty Questions, I Spy and Car Snooker. Also it turned out she was awesome at 'Would You Rather . . . ?' She'd ask things like, 'Would you rather live in a whale's blow-hole or a kangaroo's pouch?' or 'Would you rather have hands that stank of cheese or breath that stank of old fish?' and I'd have to pick one. Brilliant.

In between games we talked about all sorts of stuff – football, school, food, her crazy grandma in India, *everything*. I'd never chatted to Vanya for this long before and it was the happiest I'd felt all week. The nuggets had helped me make a new friend! And a really nice, normal one at that.

In contrast, Gamble spent most of the journey trying to make Kevin throw up by tickling his belly and telling him disgusting stories, like the time he sprinkled dried scabs into his brother Spud's lasagne, or how his dog Scratchy once ate his auntie's glass eye and they had to wait three days for it to . . . ahem . . . *pass through*. Apparently she still wears it, which is even more gross.

Amazingly Kevin managed to keep his breakfast down, which was a record for him. When Gamble finally got bored, he prowled up the coach, past

Mr Noblet (who was by now fast asleep), to where Vanya and I were sitting.

'Come back, Darren,' yawned Miss Clegg but Gamble ignored her so she went back to playing with her phone.

'Budge up,' said Gamble, pushing Vanya along and perching on the edge of the seat with his carrier bag on his lap. 'D'you want your treat now, Roman?'

'Hmmm . . . maybe later,' I said. Now I knew that the treat wasn't a doughnut there wasn't much point in having it.

Gamble sniffed. 'Wanna set off a stink bomb, then?'

'Why would we do that?' said Vanya, frowning. 'We're all stuck on the same bus.'

'Cos it's funny, innit,' tutted Gamble. 'And who asked you anyway, bog brush?'

Vanya sighed.

'We could shave off Mr Noblet's moustache with my pen-knife while he's sleeping,' said Gamble, excitedly.

I looked at Vanya, who rolled her eyes. I felt so embarrassed – here I was trying to make a new friend and Gamble was ruining everything. Gamble was jerking his head around. I'd seen him do this before, it means he's bored and looking for something to do. When he's like this, anything can happen.

'Hey! Listen to this,' he said, pulling *1001 Amazing and Disgusting Facts for Kids* out of his bag and flipping to a random page. 'In America a man once married his horse.'

'Wow. Fascinating,' said Vanya, looking out of the window.

Gamble doesn't understand sarcasm, though. He just ploughed straight on. And on. And on. 'And the Romans used to brush their teeth with wee and someone once made a piano out of live cats and . . .'

We were then treated to ten minutes non-stop of the world's most tattooed dog, and the loudest ever burp, and two-headed dolphins until . . .

' . . . and you can lead a cow upstairs but you can't . . . Hey, look! That lorry driver's waving at us!'

Now, although I was pretty bored of hearing Gamble's facts, I *do* wish that he'd got to the end of that one about cows.

Firstly, he'd missed the second half of the fact. This meant we didn't hear the key bit of information that could have saved us a great deal of trauma at the end of our class trip. But I'll save that until later.

And secondly, well, what happened next was absolutely vile. Most people would just wave back at a driver who was waving at them, or even pull a funny face. Not Darren Gamble.

Before I could do anything, he'd scrambled up so he was standing on my legs, his shorts were round his ankles and his bum was pressed against the window. 'Come on everyone!' he called to the rest of the bus. 'Moony!'

Oh, it was horrible. His scrawny bottom was waggling around inches from my face. I couldn't fight him off because he was holding onto the seats. I couldn't scream because then my open mouth would be touching his spotty buttocks. There was nothing I could do. I was stuck. Behind me I could hear Rosie Taylor squealing that *I* was disgusting, like I'd *chosen* to have Gamble's rear end next to my head.

Luckily, I had Vanya.

I told you she was a karate black belt, didn't I?

I'm not sure exactly what happened next. Somehow, though, Gamble somersaulted through the air. The next thing I knew he was face down in the aisle, howling in pain as Vanya twisted his arm up behind his back.

'Darren, stop doing that, whatever it is,' said Miss Clegg, without turning around.

Vanya let go of him and Gamble skulked back to his seat, pulling up his shorts and grumbling that it wasn't fair 'cos he wasn't allowed to hit girls.

Vanya plonked herself back down next to me and blew a strand of hair out of her face. 'So, remind me, *why* are you friends with him?' she said.

I said nothing. Maybe she had a point.

Ah, We're Here

After pulling off the motorway, we travelled for a few miles along a twisty, turny country road. Amazingly, Kevin 'Pukelear Missile' Harrison *still* didn't throw up. Vanya was just as chatty as ever but I noticed that, up ahead, Gamble was very quiet.

Eventually, the coach turned into a long driveway and everybody cheered. There were two signs at the end of the drive. One read: 'Cloud Farm,

Livestock and Dairy', with a picture of sheep, cows, horses and chickens underneath it. The other sign said: 'Farm View Outdoor Survival Centre – Where Only The Strongest Will Survive'.

I gulped.

'Don't worry about the sign – it's a load of rubbish,' laughed Vanya, noticing the fear in my face. 'They're not going to send us anywhere dangerous, are they? It'll be fun, I promise.'

As much as I liked Vanya, I'd soon find out that she was completely wrong about that.

The driveway – a single track with grass growing down the middle – seemed to go on for ages. There was thick woodland to our right and fields full of cows and sheep on our left. A few people covered their noses and made *poooeey* noises at the stink, which was fairly ripe. I wasn't too bothered, though. Gamble is my best friend, after all – I'm used to terrible smells.

When the coach had rumbled on for about half a mile, the driveway split in two. The left turn led towards a large farmhouse and a couple of huge barns with cars and tractors parked outside. We followed the right-hand fork, which took us along a bumpy track through the dark woods.

The coach negotiated a couple of tight bends then we suddenly burst out into the sunshine. Everyone cheered again as we stopped in a small car park. Mr Noblet shook himself awake. 'Ah, we're here,' he said. I wasn't sure if he'd actually been asleep or if he'd been pretending so he didn't have to deal with Gamble. He stood up and cleared his throat. 'OK, guys, go over to the picnic area. Enjoy your lunch. Miss Clegg – will you be sitting with Darren?'

'Wouldn't have thought so,' said Miss Clegg, who'd made her way down the aisle. 'Anyway. I need the loo. Long journeys play havoc with my guts.'

Lovely.

'It *is* kind of your job . . . ' began Mr Noblet but Miss Clegg interrupted him.

'Look. I sat with him all the way here, didn't I?' she said sourly. 'What more do you want from me? Blood?'

Mr Noblet's mouth dropped open as Miss Clegg bustled down the stairs and into the little toilet. I guess she wasn't that happy to be on residential with us.

Meanwhile the rest of us all piled off the coach

and blinked against the sunlight. We stepped directly out onto a picnic area and an adventure playground with nets, slides and climbing frames next to a couple of trampolines sunk into the ground. At the edge of the playground was a huge wooden platform, easily as tall as a house. There was a zip wire leading from the top of it, down a steep hill between the trees to another platform about a hundred metres away.

The zip wire looked awesome. Completely terrifying, but awesome.

'I can't wait to go on that!' said Vanya, clapping her hands, 'But first . . . you owe me some chicken nuggets!'

Lunch

There was nobody from the centre there to meet us. This seemed a bit weird but Mr Noblet told us to sit and eat, and he was sure that someone would be along soon.

Vanya and I sat down on a picnic bench and swapped lunchboxes. My mouth was already watering. I was just about to fling the lid off and gobble down the doughnut when Kevin 'The

Pukelear Missile' Harrison wandered over. He tried to sit down next to Rosie Taylor on the next table but she told him she'd 'rather be sneezed on by a giant slug' than sit next to him, which wasn't very kind. Disappointed, he looked around for somewhere else to eat.

'Hey, Kev,' said Vanya. 'Come sit with us.'

Wow! What a nice person. I'm not really used to having nice friends. Gamble's idea of being nice is twisting *both* of your nipples so they go a matching shade of purple.

Vanya smiled at Kevin as he plonked himself down. 'I noticed the travel-sickness wristbands worked.'

This seemed to perk Kevin up a bit. He wiggled his wrists at us, showing us the two grey bands that were round each one. 'Thanks for lending them to me, Vanya. You were right – two sets of bands *did* work. First time ever I've been on a coach without puking up. I feel great!' he said, wrenching the top of his lunchbox off. It was absolutely stuffed full of grub.

A moment later, Gamble sat down uninvited and started nosing round our food like a rat at the bins. 'Who wants to swap then?' He was holding up his cheese sandwich to try and entice us.

Best friend or not, there was no way he was getting even a sniff of my doughnut. In any case, next to the white bread, his filthy fingers looked like something a dog might've left in the snow.

'Aw, come on, Roman. Cheese butty for whatever you've got,' he whined. 'I've got a treat hidden in my bag for you, remember?'

'Hmmm,' I said, focusing on the lunchbox with the doughnut in it. There was no way his treat could match *that*.

Kevin wasn't keen to swap with Gamble either. He gobbled his sandwich in about three bites then followed it up with a Twix, a fairy cake and a yoghurt, before washing it all down with a full can of Dr Pepper. The whole thing took no more than thirty seconds. 'Sorry. None left,' he said, before letting out a loud, wet burp.

'Yoghurt *and* fizzy drinks?' I said, shuffling away from him. 'Are you sure that's a good mixture for you, Kevin?'

'Course,' said Kevin, 'I have 'em every day.'

'But you're sick every day too,' I replied slowly.

'Not *every* day,' sniffed Kevin. 'Anyway I've got

four wristbands on – I'm immune. Who's coming on the trampoline?'

'I really don't think so,' I replied flatly.

'Hmmm,' said Vanya, 'I'm not sure the wristbands work when y–'

Kevin waved his hand at her. 'It'll be fine. I feel awesome thanks to you, Vanya,' he said. Before she could reply he had run off to the trampolines and was bouncing up and down enthusiastically.

'That's not going to end well,' I said.

'Hey!' said Vanya, suddenly. 'Do you mind?'

While we were busy watching Kevin on the trampoline, Gamble had reached into Vanya's lunchbox, grabbed a handful of chicken nuggets and stuffed them into his mouth. Mouth open, he was now chewing them sloppily.

'You snooze you lose,' he grinned, spraying half-eaten nugget out all over the table.

'That's not fair,' said Vanya, pushing away the remaining nuggets like they were infected with a tropical disease. Knowing Gamble, this wasn't totally impossible.

Gamble swallowed hard. 'It wasn't *fair* when you didn't share your lunch, or when you nearly broke my arm, *or* when you muscled in on my best mate. Me and Roman share everything, ain't that right, Roman?' said Gamble, before helping himself to two more nuggets.

I forced a smile, giving Vanya back her tuna wrap while also covering the doughnut with my hand.

Pulling the massive cup-and-straw out of his carrier bag and plonking it on the table, Gamble started smacking his lips together. 'Cor, those nuggets were really dry. Are you trying to kill me or what? My mouth's like a lizard's undies!'

'Not really my fault,' said Vanya. '*You* stole them.'

Gamble ignored her. 'I'm dying for a drink now, thanks to you,' he said, taking a huge slurp on his straw.

'What *is* that?' I said, looking uneasily at the fizzy blue stuff in the cup.

'Energy drink – *Electric Hyper*,' grinned Gamble, between gulps. 'It's illegal in some countries.'

'It's . . . what?!' I exclaimed.

'S'what our Spud said,' sniffed Gamble. 'Some kids in Greece went blind or summat. Fancy a bit?'

I looked at the straw and shook my head.

Gamble took another massive glug. 'I love it cos

it gives you a proper energy buzz so you go crazy mental then you can't sleep for two days.'

Exactly what Gamble needs – more energy.

'Oh, and the best thing is,' he said, leaning in towards me, 'it turns your wee green.'

'How splendid,' said Vanya, her face all crinkled up as if nothing could possibly be *less* splendid.

At that moment, a blood-red open-top sports car shot into the car park. It skidded to a dusty halt between the coach and the zip wire tower.

'Awesome!' said Gamble, gulping down more of the Electric Hyper.

A young man vaulted out of the sports car without opening the door. He was tall and tanned and so muscular that he was bursting out of his tight t-shirt. There was a tangle of tattoos all the way up his arms. He gave Mr Noblet a friendly pat on the shoulder that nearly knocked him over.

'Gather round, my people!' he said, removing his sunglasses. 'It's time to survive.'

Mad Dan

We all sat on the grass in front of the man, apart from Rosie Taylor, who remained standing and said,

'Fabulous people do *not* get grass stains on eighty-pound dresses, thank you very much.' I was next to Vanya and Gamble, with the doughnut lunchbox clutched to my chest. Was I ever going to get the chance to eat it? There were way too many people around.

Miss Clegg walked down the steps of the bus, wiping her hands on her trousers. When she noticed the man, she froze with her foot in mid-air. Her eyes were nearly popping out of her head, like he was made entirely out of chocolate cake.

'Mad Dan's the name,' he announced in a deep growl. 'Ex-Special Forces. Expert in survival and jungle combat. Owner of this place. You lucky people are working with me this week. Do I get an awoooga?'

He lifted his hands to his ears. As he did so, the muscles on his arms twitched, causing his tattoos to wriggle about like snakes.

'Awoooga!' screamed everyone apart from me and Vanya. I don't really like it when adults try to impress kids by shouting stupid stuff.

Vanya noticed that I'd not shouted back. 'Loves himself a bit,' she whispered.

As if to prove this, Mad Dan ran his fingers

through his swept-back hair and winked at Miss Clegg, who was so delighted she fell off the bottom step of the bus. Mad Dan leapt forward and caught her. 'Lucky I was here, hey, kitty cat?'

Miss Clegg turned bright red and laughed like a maniac as Mad Dan flipped her back to her feet.

'*Kitty cat*?' mouthed Vanya to me, before pretending to put her fingers down her throat.

I giggled even though I was mildly disgusted by the idea of him flirting with Miss Clegg. I mean, I know his name's *Mad* Dan but come on. Anyone *that* mad should probably be locked up. As well as being massive and dreary, Miss Clegg also has a pretty awful wind problem. One time she bent over to pick something up in the classroom and let rip with an absolute belter. It sounded like someone had crushed a goose.

'Got a problem?' barked Mad Dan suddenly at me and Vanya.

Mouth clamped shut, I shook my head.

'Not at all,' said Vanya, a smile playing at the corners of her mouth.

Mad Dan harrumphed then turned to face the rest of the class. 'OK, survivors. This here's the story. Your lives are gonna be at risk.'

Everyone went *ooohhh*.

'Cool,' said Gamble, missing the point slightly. His head was twitching like a mad rabbit and he was bouncing up and down so much I thought he might take off. I guessed the Electric Hyper had kicked in.

'So *bosh*,' Dan continued, punching the palm of his hand. 'You're gonna tap some mad things, people. Ten minutes time that zip line is gonna transport you to the survival zone. You've got two nights down there. Out in the wild. You're gonna learn how to fend for yourselves. Building shelters. Hunting for food. Battling nature. Trying to stay alive.'

'Will we be able to kill our own dinner?' asked Gamble.

'Apparently we're "not allowed",' said Dan, doing that speech mark thing with his fingers. Gamble looked thoroughly disappointed.

'Is there wi-fi or do I have to use mobile internet?' asked Rosie.

'I've no idea,' replied Dan. 'This is the wilderness, not a holiday camp.'

I gulped.

Vanya nudged me. 'Don't worry,' she whispered,

'I told you. It's all pretend. We're not *really* in any danger.'

I tried to smile back at her.

'Questions?' said Mad Dan, pulling a toothpick out of his pocket and chewing it.

Rosie put her hand up again. 'Nice car. That French actress, Miranda Vermin, has one just like it.'

Mad Dan ran his finger along the gleaming car bonnet. 'It's beautiful, isn't it?'

'Eh?' said Vanya. 'Bit weird.'

Dan frowned at her. 'What do you mean?'

Vanya shrugged. 'Well, I didn't think a *survival* expert would waste his time on a luxury sports car, that's all.'

'Well, if you're gonna survive, you've gotta have something worth living for,' grunted Dan, who seemed really annoyed by Vanya's question. 'But if you must know, I'd rather be hiking through a jungle or riding a wild horse any day.'

'Amazing,' said Miss Clegg breathily.

'Right,' said Vanya, rolling her eyes.

Rosie spread some lipstick on her lips. 'Well, one day I'm going to be famous so when I win an Oscar for best actress, I'll let you drive me to the awards ceremony.'

She said this like she was doing him a favour. As Mad Dan tried to think of a response, Gamble leapt to his feet, his eyes wild from the crazy blue drink. 'You said you were in the Special Forces is that like the army do you have a machine gun can you get me a go in a tank have you ever killed anyone?'

Mad Dan tapped his nose. 'Top secret, my excitable little friend. Top secret. Any more questions?'

Miss Clegg put her hand up. For once, she didn't look or sound like she was about to fall asleep. 'Er . . . ahem . . . where do *you* live?'

Mad Dan waved his hand towards the bottom of the hill. 'I sleep in the trees down there. In a shelter I made out of logs and branches. My roof is the sky and my carpet is the forest floor. And my bath . . . well, I wash myself in the lake. I'll show you if you like.'

Miss Clegg looked she was about to explode.

'Steady on,' said Mr Noblet.

Mad Dan laughed. 'I mean the shelter. I'll show you the shelter.'

Miss Clegg actually looked a bit disappointed.

'Incredible how he gets his hair so perfect, even

though he lives in the forest,' whispered Vanya to me. 'Still – all part of the act, I suppose.'

Vanya was right – there was something a bit strange about him that nobody else seemed to notice. He looked way too clean and neat to sleep outside.

'OK, *bosh*,' said Mad Dan. 'T-minus eight minutes we hit the zip wire. Enjoy the rest of your meal and your freedom. Cut loose on the play-ground and in the woods. But, people, we've got two rules here at Farm View. One: stay alive. And two: never – *and I mean never* – cross the fence and go into the farm. Give me an awooga if you've got that.'

'Awooga!' replied everyone.

'Why can't we go in the farm?' asked Gamble, blinking hard. 'I love farms, me.'

'Is that because the animals have similar toilet habits to you?' said Rosie.

'Shut it you manky bum canoe,' said Gamble.

I've no idea what this insult meant but it somehow seemed to fit her perfectly.

Mad Dan pointed a huge finger at Gamble. 'Farm's out of bounds. Go there and bad things will happen. Trust me. Right. At ease, people.'

Whilst Mad Dan was grabbing some ropes and harnesses out of his car boot, Mr Noblet went over to Miss Clegg. 'Have you checked there's nothing left on the coach?'

Miss Clegg was staring dreamily at Mad Dan. 'Sure. I've Dan that. I mean *done* that.'

Heavenly Delight

Back at the picnic table, Gamble was guzzling more and more of the Electric Hyper. He was now speaking super-fast and his eyes were bulging like footballs.

'Maybe you shouldn't drink any more of that stuff,' I said to him.

Gamble shivered. His lips and tongue were bright blue. 'No, see, cos what it is, right, I'm well thirsty after them nuggets so it's not my fault, innit, you gotta blame the nuggets.'

'You're *sweating* quite a lot,' I said. It was pouring down his face and neck.

'Oh wow! You're right,' panted Gamble, dabbing his face with his shirt. 'I'm like cheese under a grill here!'

He pulled a tissue out of his pocket and wiped

his armpits with it. There was a large wheelie bin next to the picnic table and he lifted the lid and dropped the tissue in.

'Disgusting!' sneered Rosie Taylor from the next table.

'Shut it or I'll smash you one, you massive pig's nipple,' replied Gamble, clanging the lid of the wheelie bin down again.

'Ooh, I'm *soooo* scared,' said Rosie, nodding towards Vanya with a smirk. 'I saw you getting beaten up on the bus by a girl, remember.'

At this, Gamble's lips went tight and his head began jerking uncontrollably. This was not a good sign.

Meanwhile, Kevin wasn't looking good either. He was bent double, clutching his stomach. 'Urrgh,' he groaned. 'My belly feels like a custard whirlpool.'

'Well, you did eat all that food then go on the tram–' I began but Kevin interrupted.

'No,' he said, 'I just need something to settle my stomach. Here, Vanya. Give us one of them nuggets.'

Before she could tell him she only had two left, he'd plunged his hand into the lunchbox and snatched one. 'That's better,' he said between chews. 'I'll definitely be OK now.'

I inched away from him. As far as I could see, eating more food to stop himself being sick was like pumping more air into a balloon to stop it from bursting.

'Well, if he's having one, I will,' said Gamble, pinching the last one in the box. He didn't eat it, though. There was a weird, scary glint in his eyes like he was planning something terrible, and he was fiddling with the lid of his cup.

So, as you can tell, it was not exactly a relaxing lunch. Still, with everyone else busy either eating or playing on the playground, this was my big chance. I tried to put all the craziness to one side. After all, I had a doughnut to enjoy, and T-minus four minutes to eat it.

I looked around me then eased the lunchbox open. A waft of sweetness instantly shot up my nostrils. My tongue began to tingle. I lifted the gorgeous doughnut towards my mouth and prepared to bite into it.

Thanks to the chicken nuggets, I'd made a new friend *and* I'd managed to get hold of my favourite food. From that moment on my life would be perfect and nothing bad would ever happen to me again . . .

Or maybe not.

You see, I told you that chicken nuggets were sneaky. They'd let me think that everything was OK; they'd waited until my guard was down before they attacked. And that's the secret of a perfect ambush.

The doughnut never even made it to my mouth.

Remember when I said that Gamble looked like he was planning something terrible?

As I was raising the doughnut to my lips, Gamble was pulling the straw out of his cup. Then he stabbed it into the chicken nugget that was in his other hand. With a chunk of nugget stuck in the end of the straw, he pointed it at Rosie Taylor and blew hard in the other end. The little lump of chicken shot through the air like a torpedo and smacked her on the back of the neck.

'Bullseye!' he cackled, bouncing up and down with excitement.

'AAAAARRRGHHH!' screamed Rosie, spinning round and clutching her neck. She was about to yell at Gamble but then she saw what was in my hand. 'O–M– flipping –G! Look what Roman's got!'

I shoved the doughnut back into my lunchbox but

it was too late. Mr Noblet had already jogged over, his face concerned. 'What's wrong, Rosie?' he asked.

Rosie could barely breathe. 'It's a . . . it's a . . .' she gasped theatrically, 'it's a doughnut!'

'Oh,' said Mr Noblet. 'I thought you'd been bitten by a snake or something.'

Rosie glared at me like something she'd found wriggling in a nit comb. 'He's tormenting me with it, Mr Noblet. He knows I'm terrified of them. I'm going to need counselling after this.'

'*Bit* over-dramatic,' said Vanya from the other side of the table. 'It's just a doughnut.'

'You would say that!' snapped Rosie. 'You're friends with it.'

I realised that by 'it', she meant me.

'Where did you get the doughnut, Roman?' said Mr Noblet, calmly.

I glanced at Vanya, who opened her mouth as if to own up to it. But a deal's a deal, and I didn't want Vanya to get punished for swapping with me – she'd been so cool today and I really liked her company. So I made my decision. 'I brought it myself.'

'Make him get rid of it,' growled Rosie at Mr Noblet. 'Either the doughnut goes or I do.'

Mr Noblet sighed and nodded towards the wheelie bin. 'Well . . . rules are rules, I'm afraid, Roman. You know what to do.'

Typical. I huffed out my cheeks, pulled the sticky doughnut out of the lunchbox and dragged my feet over to the bin. In fact, I dragged them so much that a stone got into my trainer and dug into my foot. 'Ow!' I said.

'He's faking,' said Rosie.

Muttering under my breath, I dropped the doughnut into the wheelie bin. It hit the bottom with a hollow *clang*.

'That's much better,' said Rosie, smiling triumphantly and pulling out her phone. 'I'd better let the world know I'm OK. Twitter will go into meltdown if it finds out I've been exposed to a doughnut.'

'Are you supposed to have your ph–' began Mr Noblet but he was interrupted by Mad Dan.

'OK, people,' he called from the top of the zip line tower. 'Let's move. It's survival time. Leave your luggage. I'll collect it for you later.'

I paused to get the stone out of my shoe but Mr Noblet clapped his hands to urge me on. 'Come on, Roman. Do it on the stairs. Time to move. The fun starts here!'

Just before I limped to the tower I took one last despairing look at the wheelie bin. I imagined my doughnut all alone at the bottom of it, nestled on top of Gamble's sweaty armpit tissue. It was the most depressing thought I'd ever had.

Up until then, anyway . . .

Thunk-Splash

The zip-line tower was a wooden frame with a staircase zig-zagging up the inside of it. After hobbling over, I paused at the bottom, hoping to remove the stone from my shoe. Before I could even take my shoe off, though, Gamble grabbed my arm and dragged me hopping up the three flights of stairs.

'Gotta get there first!' he panted. The Electric Hyper was *really* kicking in now.

The platform at the top was only big enough for six people and I found myself up there with Mad Dan, Gamble, Vanya, Miss Clegg (who'd sprinted up like a cheetah after Mad Dan) and Kevin 'Pukelear Missile' Harrison. There was a safety rail round three sides of the platform. The fourth side was open, with the zip wire stretching off into the distance.

I edged away from that side and held onto the

safety rail. Mad Dan's sports car was directly below us. From up here it looked like a Matchbox toy, and the trampoline looked like a postage stamp. My tummy did a little flip so I decided not to look down again.

'This is well-mega-high, this,' said Gamble, bouncing up and down so hard that the planks of the platform shook. 'I reckon you'd splatter everywhere if you fell from here, Kev.'

Kevin peered over the top of the safety rail then drew his head back quickly. 'Yikes,' he said, taking deep breaths. I knew how he felt, and I'm pretty sure Vanya had noticed too.

'Don't listen to him,' she sighed.

Gamble put his arm round Kevin. 'We'd probably need to scrape you up off the floor. You'd look like a smashed lasagne.'

Kevin's face went white.

Handing Miss Clegg a harness, Mad Dan growled, 'Ain't nobody died on here yet.'

'You make me feel so . . . *safe*,' simpered Miss Clegg.

Yuck. To take my mind off her horrible flirting, I decided to finally remove the stone from my trainer. I bent down to untie my laces.

'I'm not very well,' said Kevin, swallowing hard.

As I stood up to shake out the stone there was a slight gust of wind.

'Did you feel the tower wobble then, oh my word it proper started rocking, I reckon it's gonna fall over,' sniggered Gamble. Amazingly he made this sound like it was a good thing.

Mouth clamped shut, Kevin shook his head.

Gamble ruffled Kevin's hair. 'This is ace, it's swaying in the wind, we're all gonna die, hahaha!'

Suddenly, Kevin's eyes opened wide. His cheeks swelled out and his hand slapped onto his mouth. Then he leapt at me and grabbed the trainer out of my hand. Before I could stop him, he'd buried his face in it and made a loud, disgusting *flaaaaarg-gggh* noise.

'That's my trainer!' I howled.

'Sorry, Roman,' groaned Kevin, wiping his chin against his shoulder. 'It was that chicken nugget I ate. It tipped me over the edge.'

'Uurgh! That stinks!' cried Gamble, which was a bit rich coming from him.

Kevin held the trainer out to me, as though it was some precious gift I would really want. He looked like one of the three kings in the Christmas play: Gold, Frankincense and *Bleuuurgh*. 'Here you go,' he said kindly.

Speechless, I stared at the trainer for a moment. Why on earth would I want to take it back off him? What looked like really chunky vegetable soup was slopping about inside and oozing through the holes for the laces.

Without warning, Gamble yanked my trainer off Kevin, flung it over the edge of the platform then dusted off his hands. 'Ah. That's better.'

From far below there was a loud *thunk-splash* noise, followed by the sound of a car alarm going off.

'My car!' yelled Mad Dan, desperately leaning over the safety rail.

Tremendous.

We all crowded round to look. Far below us, my trainer was lying in the middle of Dan's car bonnet. It was surrounded by a massive, multi-coloured puddle. There must've been gallons of the stuff! Seriously – it looked like he'd ram-raided a yoghurt factory.

Mad Dan slapped both hands down on the safety rail and turned to Kevin. 'You've ruined my beautiful car, you vomiting imbecile!'

Bit harsh, I thought, *but ultimately true*.

Shocked at this sudden outburst, everyone shuffled back a bit. Kevin began to sob.

'Er . . . ahem,' said Vanya coolly. 'That's not very nice, Dan. Kevin is sick. I thought a *survival* expert would make sure people were OK before he worried about his car.'

Wow! I'd never speak to an adult like that. It was becoming increasingly clear that Vanya might be nice but she was also tough.

Mad Dan took a deep breath and looked up into the air. Then he forced a smile. When he spoke, his teeth were locked together and angry red blotches were appearing on his cheeks. 'Yo, whatever. Is the little dude OK?'

Kevin nodded sadly. 'It happens a lot.'

'I'm worried about birds or squirrels eating the sick and getting poisoned, see?' said Mad Dan.

'Right,' said Vanya, who didn't seem convinced.

Mad Dan ran his fingers through his hair. 'Look. Just make sure it gets clean. There's a tap and a hose at the edge of the car park. You three can miss the zip wire and walk down after.'

He pointed at me, Kevin and Gamble.

'What?! You're kidding – that's well shady,' protested Gamble.

Kevin actually looked pretty pleased.

Miss Clegg smiled sweetly at Mad Dan whilst grabbing Gamble a little bit too tightly by the hand. 'I'll make sure it's *sparkling*, Daniel.'

'Awooga, babe,' said Mad Dan, cheering up instantly and winking at her. 'Here's my car keys. You'll find sponges and buckets in the boot.'

So Gamble, Kevin and I had to traipse back down the stairs past the rest of our class. Then we had to listen to everyone screaming with excitement as they shot down the zip line one by one whilst we scrubbed half-digested lumps of Kevin's lunch off Mad Dan's car.

What a terrific start to the residential.

And it was all the fault of the chicken nuggets. Well, mainly, anyway. If Gamble hadn't eaten them, he might not have drunk all that Electric Hyper. Then he might not have fired a chicken nugget cannon ball at Rosie and cost me my doughnut, or got quite so excitable at the top of the platform with Kevin. And, along with deranged Gamble, maybe that extra nugget *had* tipped Kevin over the edge.

Yes. The nuggets had well and truly ambushed me. But this wasn't a one-off attack. Oh no. They would keep on pummelling me until they'd completely crushed my spirit.

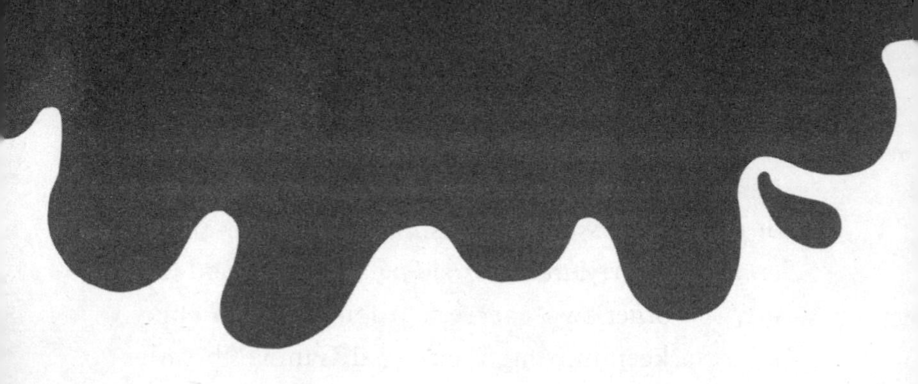

Afternoon

When I Had to Survive a Near-Drowning, and Mr Noblet Had to Survive a Mouthful of Nugget

I suppose the one good thing about Gamble drinking the Electric Hyper was that he had tonnes of energy to clean the car. In fact, he was scrubbing so hard that Kevin and I barely had to do anything. I was able to hop over to the big pile of luggage and find my case. I opened it up and grabbed my wellies so at least I could wear something on my feet.

'Come on, boys. Make it shine. Nothing but the best for Dan,' said Miss Clegg. She was slapping on make-up and admiring herself in a small mirror. I don't want to be nasty but this was a bit of a waste of time. I mean, you wouldn't bother painting your house if it looked like it was about to fall down, would you?

'Don't worry, miss, I'm doing a proper good job, me, the other two can rest, I don't mind, I enjoy it, gotta keep moving, innit,' said Gamble, breathlessly, from the other side of the car. He was spraying the hose with one hand whilst his other hand was a total blur.

Kevin and I didn't need to be asked twice. We wandered back to the picnic table and sat there playing Top Trumps for almost an hour, until Gamble cried, 'Done!'

Kevin, Miss Clegg and I went over to admire his handiwork. I have to say that the car looked amazing – all glistening and shiny like it was brand-new.

'Wow! Dan will be pleased with me,' said Miss Clegg, her face covered in so much make-up she looked like she'd been kissing a clown. 'Er . . . and *you,* of course, Darren. How did you get it so clean?'

Darren puffed out his cheeks and stretched. 'Hard work and the right tools,' he said. 'Same as what my uncle says you need for a good robbery.'

Gamble's uncle is currently in prison for robbing our local shop. I was just thinking about this when I noticed what Gamble was holding in his hand. *Hang on!* My eyes flicked towards the luggage. My case was open. I could've sworn I'd zipped it up after fetching my wellies. It felt like ice crystals formed in my blood as I realised what he'd done. I shouldn't have taken my eyes off him for a second . . .

In Gamble's hand was a toothbrush. Or, to be more precise, *my* toothbrush. The bristles were all black and splayed out and there were strange bits of *stuff* stuck to them.

'What are you doing with that?' I asked, trying to keep my voice calm.

Gamble looked at the toothbrush then at me, like I was asking a really stupid question. 'Getting the crusty bits of sick out of the tyres. They're proper stubborn, innit.'

'But why are you using *my* toothbrush?'

Gamble frowned. 'Cos I didn't bring one,' he said, as if this was the most obvious thing in the world. 'Should I put it back in your bag? I used your towel as well.'

My towel was lying in a filthy heap in a puddle.

I know it was just an old one that Mum had chucked in the case but come on!

'No,' I sighed. 'You might as well put them both straight in the bin.'

Perfect.

Trudge

From the car park, it should've been a couple of minutes' trudge along the woodland path down to the campsite. It took a lot longer, though, because Gamble kept running off into the trees, chasing after squirrels that were 'looking at him funny'. After a while, Mad Dan zoomed up behind us on a quad bike. He was towing a trailer with all our luggage on it.

'Awooga, dudes! Car's looking great!' called Mad Dan, pulling over on the path. He seemed a lot happier. 'Fancy a lift, sweetheart?'

Miss Clegg giggled like a tickled baby and hopped aboard, wrapping her arms round Mad Dan's waist. With a roar of the engine and a cheeky wave, they bounced off down the path.

Thanks a bunch.

About ten minutes later, Kevin, Gamble and I finally

reached the campsite. We found the rest of our class putting up large blue dome tents in groups of four or five. There were also two red tents already up, which I guessed were for Mr Noblet and Miss Clegg.

The campsite itself was pretty cool. It was a grassy clearing in the woods, about half the size of a football pitch. There was a white building at the far end that looked like a toilet block. Well-trodden paths led off between the trees, with wooden signs pointing to the lake, the games field, the climbing wall, the canteen, the fire pit and so on.

Mad Dan strode over to us with Miss Clegg waddling behind him like a giant duckling following its mother.

He dropped a long, bulky blue bag on the floor and thrust a rubber mallet into Gamble's hand. This was clearly a silly thing to do – Gamble and weapons don't mix. 'Right. Because of . . . what you did, you three missed the chance to choose your groups so you'll be sharing a tent together.'

'Yesssss!' said Gamble, ruffling my hair.

I looked from Gamble to Kevin and back again. 'Great,' I said flatly. Stuck in a tent for two nights with a hyperactive nutter and a constant thrower-upper. What could possibly go wrong?

Mad Dan continued, sounding as though he was still pretty cheesed off about the car. 'First rule of survival? Find shelter. You gotta build a tent. Now you weren't around for the demo but the instructions are here . . .'

He handed me a piece of paper and I scanned it.

'Is this . . . in *Chinese*?' I asked, scratching my head at the squiggles on the page.

'Correct-o-mundo,' Mad Dan said. 'I ran out of English tents. Anyway, beggars can't be choosers in a survival situation. You've gotta make do. After all, your life could depend on it.'

You've Done Well

Well, one thing's for certain. If our lives depended on building a tent then Kevin, Gamble and I would definitely be dead.

Kevin curled up in a ball on the floor groaning that the smell of the tent bag was making him feel ill again. Meanwhile, Gamble guzzled down the rest of his Electric Hyper, which made him even crazier than before. I had to stop him from using his pen-knife to cut windows in the canvas before we'd even got it out of the bag. After that, he marauded round the campsite, swinging the mallet round his head and yelling, 'I'm a Viking!'

Miss Clegg was too busy following Mad Dan around to help so I was left to put the tent up on my own. I soon learned that this was impossible. There were all these sticks-on-string things that kind of slotted together to make ridiculously long wobbly mega-poles, and some massive bits of material that kept billowing around like parachutes in the wind. I tried to watch what everyone else was doing but this made me even more confused so in the end I just gave up and sat on a rock.

After a while Vanya came over. 'Wow! You've done well!' she laughed. Her tent was on the other side of the field, looking perfect.

I smiled. It was nice to see her. 'I wasn't allowed to pick my own group,' I said.

'Well, it could be worse – you could be sharing a tent with her . . . ' she replied, nodding over towards Rosie Taylor, who was haranguing Mr Noblet a few metres away from us.

'I can't believe you expect me to use the same toilet as other people,' Rosie snarled, jabbing her finger at him. Even from here I could see the angry red welt on her neck where Gamble had hit her with the chicken nugget. I have to say that this did make me smile.

'Well . . . everybody has to sh–' began Mr Noblet but she cut him off.

'And there's nowhere in that stupid tent to plug in my hair straighteners,' she snapped. 'Trust me, I am *not* looking like a frizz-bomb on the photos. Imagine if they got leaked to the gossip magazines.'

'Do you really *need* hair straighteners, Rosie?' said Mr Noblet. 'Farm View is an outdoor survival centre. You'll be climbing and rafting and crawling through mud all week.'

'Mud?' said Rosie, peering over the top of her sunglasses. 'If you'd seen my Instagram profile you'd know already: Rosie Taylor does not *do* mud. And by the way, how exactly do you expect me to charge my phone?'

Mr Noblet coughed. 'Now, about your phone. You weren't meant to bring it. There *was* a letter.'

'Oh please,' said Rosie, pursing her lips. 'If I don't update my followers for three days the internet will literally explode.'

Mr Noblet seemed to be trying to work out an answer to this when Mad Dan blew a whistle.

'Dudes. Time's up. Those of you who aren't finished – that's survival, I'm afraid, a life and death race against time. Get your luggage in the tents then let's blast the first activity!'

'I'll help you with the tent later,' said Vanya, smiling at me.

Zorbing

We followed Mad Dan through the woods. I walked with Vanya. Behind me, Gamble was nattering non-stop at Miss Clegg and bouncing around like an excited monkey. 'Do you fancy Mad Dan then, miss? I think he might be a bit young for you, miss. Maybe you should go for someone your own age like Mr Noblet or my granddad, miss.'

'I'm only twenty-nine, I'll have you know,' said Miss Clegg.

'Whatever you say, miss, but I can still set you up with my granddad, miss, he's got all his own teeth and he changes his socks pretty much every day . . . '

Miss Clegg seemed more interested in gazing at Mad Dan, though. There was a funny look on her face, like she was dreaming about Fruit Pastilles.

Eventually we reached a small lake. Shimmering beneath the hot sun, the water looked cool and inviting. Several kayaks were propped up in a row against the side of a shed, and four very large transparent plastic balls were floating on the edge of the water. Each of the balls was about three metres across. They were tied to stakes that had been driven into the little sandy beach.

'Yo, my people,' announced Mad Dan, 'let me hear an aiieeee if you wanna walk on water!'

Everyone *aiieeee-d* back at him then he began his safety talk. 'OK, guys. In a survival situation, once you've got shelter you gotta decide – do I stay where I am or do I go find somewhere better? So what are you gonna do? Stay or go?'

He put his hand to his ear for us to answer.

'Go!' cried everyone.

'I've got to go!' shouted Gamble.

'Great,' said Mad Dan. 'So if you're gonna survive in the wild, you need to be able to conquer whatever we're faced with. We're gonna learn different ways of moving around this week. And the first way is this . . . water zorbing.'

He slapped one of the giant balls.

'Yeah,' whispered Vanya in my ear, 'cos whenever

you're lost in the wilderness you'll always find a giant plastic ball to get around in.'

I sniggered.

'What's that?' said Dan, angrily. 'Survival ain't funny. It's a serious business.'

I gulped. Vanya shrugged calmly. 'Nothing.'

Dan narrowed his eyes at us then continued his talk. We'd have to climb inside the ball with a partner then run about like giant aqua-hamsters on top of the water. OK, so it *was* completely stupid to pretend that this was a way of surviving in the wild. But I have to say it did look like fun!

Mad Dan clapped his hands together. 'Questions?'

Looking completely bored, Rosie Taylor put her hand up. 'Can I do it in high heels?'

Mad Dan shook his head. 'No way, Jose. You could pop the zorb. You'll have to go barefoot.'

'Hashtag – gross-gusting,' said Rosie. 'If I catch verrucas it'll be the end of my shoe-modelling career! No thanks.'

With that she scuttled off and sat on a bench. Mr Noblet went over but she turned her head away and held the palm of her hand up to him. Frustrated, he took a deep breath and ambled back over to the group.

'Anything else?' asked Mad Dan.

Miss Clegg put her hand up. 'Will you be my partner, Daniel?' she said. Her voice was all weird and throaty, like she had a gob full of sand.

'I'd love to, babe, but I've gotta stay on the side. We can hang out here if you like,' he said, winking at her.

Bleurgh!

Then he slapped one of the zorbs. 'Right. Who's first into this bad boy?'

'I've gotta go,' repeated Gamble before anyone else could answer.

I noticed that he was hopping from one leg to the other and wincing like he was in pain. Before I could ask him what was wrong, Gamble was already halfway through the narrow slit in the ball, dragging me in behind him.

Great! Not only did I have to share a tent with Gamble, now I had to do activities with him as well. I had been hoping to work with Vanya.

'Hmmm,' said Mad Dan, peering in at us. 'Two of the car-wreckers, eh?'

'Sorry,' I said.

Mad Dan grunted a slightly huffy, 'Whatever.' Without any further instruction, he pulled up the zip to close us inside. Then, after pumping in some air through the nozzle of a kind of reverse vacuum cleaner, he unclipped the rope and pushed us out onto the lake.

The zorb rolled forward and bobbed up and down, causing us to fall flat on our faces. It didn't hurt, though. It was actually pretty funny.

We helped each other to our feet and laughed as we tried to get balanced. Being inside the zorb was seriously weird – hot and stuffy with a strong plasticky smell. It was hard to stay upright and our feet sank into the sides. Beneath us we could see green water and tangled reeds.

Together, Gamble and I pressed our hands into the soft, see-through wall. Immediately we fell over again. But then we started crawling on all fours, the zorb span around and very slowly we began to move. With all his energy from the Electric Hyper, Gamble started going like the clappers and soon we were shooting across the pond. This was ace! In fact, it was the most fun I'd had in ages.

Until Gamble spoiled it, of course.

We were halfway across the lake when Gamble suddenly slowed down. Both of us flipped over onto our backs. At first I thought this was funny.

I was wrong.

'You know what,' said Gamble, 'I'm not sure I can wait any longer.'

The laughter caught in my throat. 'What do you mean, Darren?'

Gamble glanced down to his . . . *trouser area.* 'It was your fault for feeding me those chicken nuggets. I told you they were too dry. I was mega-thirsty and . . . well . . . that Electric Hyper goes right through me.'

'You need the loo? But we're trapped in a plastic ball in the middle of a lake,' I said, ignoring his crazy logic. 'Why didn't you tell anyone before we set off?'

'I did! I said "I've gotta go".'

'Then why didn't you . . . *go*?'

'What? On the shore? I'm not an animal, you know.'

I said nothing. This is a kid who once ate some cheesy *stuff* from between his toes for a dare.

'Anyway . . .' Gamble looked at his feet. 'I thought you'd get in the zorb with someone else if I left you.'

Ordinarily this might've made me feel quite sorry for him. Or good about myself. Or maybe even a little bit frightened. But there wasn't time for that now.

'Right. We've got to get back to land,' I said, clawing at the sides of the zorb.

'No,' whimpered Gamble. 'When I said "I've gotta go", I meant *right now*. Turn around.'

'What do you . . . ' I began, but then I realised what he was about to do. 'No! That's disgusting! You can't! We're stuck in here!'

'I'm sorry,' whimpered Gamble, unzipping his flies. 'But I *have* to.'

I covered my eyes and turned my head away.

There was the sound of a jet of liquid drumming against the plastic.

Gross.

'Ahhhhhh-*mazing*,' he sighed. 'Hey! Look! Told you it'd turn it green.'

This was too much. Without thinking I began scrambling away from him. Unfortunately, you can't escape when you're trapped inside a plastic ball. The zorb lurched forward. Something sloshed around my wellies. It was like being inside a nightmarish washing machine.

Behind me I heard Gamble stagger backwards and fall over.

'Stop! I've not finished yet!' he howled. 'It's going in my eyes!'

Panicking, I felt myself speeding up.

'I'm cutting us out!' yelled Gamble.

I span round. There was a flash of metal as he sliced at the wall of the zorb with his pen-knife.

'Are you insane?' I screamed but it was too late. He'd already made six or seven great big slashes in the walls. First the roof collapsed on us, then water poured in around our feet. Within seconds we were tangled up in the crumpled plastic. Warm green wee and freezing cold green lake water were slopping around all over us. It was terrible.

We began to sink.

'Help!' I screamed. 'We're going to drown!'

So Brave

We didn't drown.

Two things saved our lives. Firstly, just after I'd said we were going to drown, I landed on the lake bottom. The lake was only about knee-deep! We must've looked like a right pair of chumps – standing there in a puddle wrapped up in a giant floppy plastic bag.

Secondly, now that he'd stopped weeing everywhere, Gamble went into overdrive. A few more flashes of the knife and we were out in the fresh air.

'I've got to rescue you!' he cried, flinging the knife into the lake. Then he knocked me over and attempted to swim back to the side, lugging me behind him by the neck.

This was seriously annoying. I was pretty wet to start with but now I was completely soaked to the skin. 'Leave me alone! I can walk!' I spluttered, as he hauled me across the slimy lake bottom.

'I'm coming!' Mad Dan called, sprinting into the water and scooping us both up before carrying us to the shore under his arms. When he'd plopped us on the side, everyone who was still waiting for their turn surrounded us. My clothes were stuck to my body and I was shivering hard, despite the hot weather.

'Are you OK?' asked Mr Noblet.

'Yeah, thanks to me,' said Gamble.

I didn't respond.

'You were so brave,' said Miss Clegg.

'Cheers,' said Gamble.

Miss Clegg pursed her lips. 'I was talking to Dan.'

Mad Dan whipped off his wet t-shirt. All he had on underneath was a vest. When Miss Clegg copped an eyeful of his muscles, she made a gurgling sound like a blocked toilet.

Making sure he flexed his massive biceps, Mad Dan tossed his shirt onto a rock to dry. 'First my car, now the zorb. How did you manage to destroy it?'

He mustn't have seen Gamble's pen-knife, which was obviously a good thing. But how were we going to explain? We needed an excellent excuse. My mind was blank. I looked hopefully at Gamble. He's always lying – surely he'd be able to come up with a good reason.

Gamble scratched his head. 'I dunno. Maybe we hit a hedgehog or summat.'

'A *hedgehog*?' said Mad Dan, incredulous. 'Do they live in ponds?'

I slapped my hand over my eyes.

'No,' said Gamble, 'but that's why we hit it, see. We weren't expecting it. It was windsurfing. Or actually, maybe we were attacked by a fish with sharp fingernails . . . '

Nobody said anything for a moment or two.

'Well,' said Mr Noblet. 'The zorb must've been

faulty. The main thing is that everyone's fine. Well done to you, Darren, for saving Roman's life . . .'

Gamble celebrated by twerking aggressively.

Mad Dan stared at us, grinding his teeth together. I remained silent. No matter what I did, it seemed I couldn't help myself from making him angry.

After a moment Mr Noblet clapped his hands. 'Right, Miss Clegg. Will you escort Darren and Roman to their tent?'

Miss Clegg took a sideways glance at Dan's muscly arms. 'I think I should stay here . . . '

Mad Dan cheered up immediately. He clicked his fingers and pointed at her. 'Sweet.'

Nice One

Thanks to the sunshine, our clothes were no longer wet by the time we reached the flattened tent. Gamble said this was awesome because he 'wouldn't need a wash now.' (I'll just remind you he was covered in dried wee and pond water. Seriously, he stank like a tuna baguette that'd been left behind a radiator for a month.)

However, because I'm not a revolting animal, I did have a shower in the toilet block. It was icy cold.

Unfortunately I'd had to bin my towel so Gamble had to lend me his flannel to dry myself with. It was only *after* I'd used it that he casually informed me that he normally uses this flannel to clean his pet dog Scratchy (yes, the one with bum worms).

This revelation meant I was forced to have a second mega-long skin-scraping scrub under the shower. Afterwards there was nothing to dry myself with except toilet paper, which is completely useless for drying a human body because it just falls to bits and gets stuck *everywhere*. It took ages. I was surprised to find Gamble waiting for me back at the tent, reading his fact book. He said he didn't want to work with anyone but me so he wasn't going back until I was ready. This was both sweet and scary in equal measure.

In any case, we'd taken so long that we ended up missing the next activity, which was 'recognising edible plants'. This sounded totally boring so I wasn't actually too bothered about skipping it anyway; I mean, what kind of a lunatic would actually *eat* a plant?

So, at four o'clock, Gamble and I met everyone else for free time on the games pitch. The pitch was a rough patch of grass right at the edge of the Farm

View site, which had a couple of old football goals and a moth-eaten volleyball net. About ten metres behind one of the goals was a low wooden fence that separated the survival centre from the farm. On the other side of the fence was a small, empty field with the farm buildings beyond it. Along the fence were handwritten signs saying 'KEEP OUT!' and 'Beware of the Animals' and all that kind of stuff.

A few people were sitting around on the grass chatting and there was a football game in progress. Gamble instantly ran over and rugby-tackled someone who didn't even have the ball. Vanya waved to me from the pitch. 'Come and join in!' she called, whilst completing an expert back-heel to a team-mate.

'I'm wearing wellies,' I replied, pointing at my feet. I'm also pretty much the worst footballer of all time.

'Doesn't matter!' she shouted. 'You can be on my team.'

And so, reluctantly, I joined in. It was alright too. In fact, I played better than I've ever played before. I mean, I didn't score any goals, or make any decent passes, or actually even touch the ball.

But still, I didn't completely embarrass myself either.

For a while, at least.

After about ten minutes, I was hanging around in front of the opposition goal hoping that the ball might bounce off me and go in at some point. Out on the wing, Vanya glided past three players, dropped her shoulder to dodge round the last defender then sent in a perfect cross. I leapt up in the air like a salmon, brought back my head to plant the ball in the bottom corner, then . . .

Crunch!

Two feet crashed into my spine and I flew forward, smashing chest-first into the post before rebounding onto the grass.

'Penalty!' cried Vanya.

'Sorry, mate,' said Gamble, untangling himself from me. 'I was going for the ball.'

'Well, you only missed it by about three metres,' I groaned. Just because Darren's my best mate, it doesn't mean he won't try to snap me in half occasionally.

Vanya picked up the ball and put it on the penalty spot. 'Go on, Roman. You take it.'

I peeled myself off the floor and stretched out my back. 'Are you sure?'

'Definitely. You can do it!' she grinned.

Her belief in me gave me a surge of confidence. After limping over to the spot, I took a few deep breaths to compose myself. Then, with a short run-up, I belted the ball as hard as I could. It rocketed through the air, straight past the keeper's despairing dive, and into the roof of the net.

Of course, by 'it', I mean my welly.

The ball, however, followed a very different path. It flew about three miles over the goal. In fact it was still rising as it sailed over the top of the fence before bouncing a few times in the farmer's field then disappearing under a tractor by the barn.

'Nice one, Ronaldo,' cackled Rosie, who was watching from the sidelines. 'Good luck getting that back!'

Watched

I didn't want to go and get the ball. I mean, I know that the field was empty, and there was nobody about, but still, it felt really wrong. Mad Dan had told us that we had to stay out. In fact it was one of his main rules and I didn't want to get into trouble. There was no point arguing with Gamble, though. He practically carried me to the fence and threw me over. Everyone else clapped their hands and chanted: 'Get it! Get it!'

'Don't worry,' urged Vanya, seeing my fear. 'It'll only take you a second. Anyway, rules are there to be broken.'

I smiled weakly back at her and sprinted across the field, dodging dried-out cow pats on the way. The ball was right underneath the front axel of the tractor so I had to lie on my back and reach for it with my feet. Just as I gripped it between my ankles and pulled it towards me, though, I got a very strange, uneasy feeling.

I was being watched.

With a big gulp, I clutched the ball to my chest and slowly turned around. What I saw nearly caused my heart to explode.

I was eyeball-to-chest with a large brown chicken.

A chicken!

Good grief! I don't know if you've ever been that close to a chicken but they are the creepiest things you will ever see in your entire life – the jerky movements, the tiny head tilted to one side, the scaly orange feet . . . Not to mention the weird red dangly bits on the forehead, the sharp, cruel beak, the cold and unblinking black eyes.

'*Bwark*!' it said, jabbing its beak inches in front of my nose.

I screamed.

Suddenly a pair of wellies came round the corner and the chicken darted away.

'Are you alright down there, dear?' said the owner of the wellies. An old-ish woman carrying a bucket was bending down to look at me. She was wearing a wax jacket and horse-riding trousers.

Without replying, I scrambled to my feet and pelted it back across the field as quickly as I could, clutching the ball under my arm. This was probably a bit rude, but I wanted to get out of there. Just as I dropped over the fence, Mad Dan came through the woods and onto the field.

'Awooga, survivors!' he announced.

We all looked back at him guiltily. I was standing next to the fence with the ball in my hands.

Dan glared at me, then at the ball. 'You didn't just go over the fence, did you?'

'Nope,' I replied.

He was about to say something else when the woman in the wellies called over from the barn. 'Yoo-hoo! Daniel!'

Mad Dan winced. For some reason he pretended not to hear her. 'Right, guys. Canteen now. Teatime. Go, go, go!' he yelled, turning round and bounding off ahead through the trees.

What a strange reaction, I thought.

By the tractor, the lady's hand dropped slowly to her waist and she trudged away sadly.

One Fussy Kid

The canteen was basically a metal roof with posts in the four corners and open sides. There were four rows of tables and benches. At one end there was a small kitchen building containing freezers and ovens, but today Dan was cooking for us outside on a gas barbeque. The smell of sausages was absolutely mouth-watering.

'Ooooh, he can cook as well,' sighed Miss Clegg, who was standing a little bit too close to his shoulder.

'OK, guys,' Mad Dan said through the smoke. 'In a survival situation, food is normally the last thing you worry about.'

What a load of rubbish, I thought. It's the first thing I worry about in any situation.

'You can survive a few weeks without food,' he continued. When he said this I laughed. It took me a moment or two to realise he wasn't joking.

'Apparently, though,' he said, 'I'm not allowed to test this out on you. So on the menu tonight are hot dogs and beans. Let me hear an awooga!'

Everyone awooga-ed. Even I was fairly excited about this. It made a change at least.

'Apart from for . . . er . . . .' He pulled a piece of paper out of his apron pocket and squinted at it. 'Roman, that is. You'll be eating chicken nuggets.'

He held up a blackened nugget from the barbeque with a pair of tongs.

My heart sank. I'd forgotten that Mum had phoned ahead. '*Can* you barbeque chicken nuggets?' I said.

'This is a survival situation,' replied Mad Dan. 'Even if all you've got to eat is tree bark and an old shoe, then that's what you eat. And anyway, I ain't firing up the deep-fat fryers for one fussy kid. You've already caused enough trouble today.'

There was a hint of coldness in his voice. Frankly, though, I think I'd have taken tree bark and a shoe over the chicken nuggets any day.

FWPAAAH!

We all queued up at the barbeque. Dan was loading the plates. Miss Clegg stood next to him, serving the beans whilst telling him how *amazing* it all smelled and how *clever* he was. Luckily she was so entranced by Dan that she slopped a ladle-full onto my plate next to my nuggets. I would have preferred one of the hot dogs or, better still, a delicious raspberry-jam filled doughnut – but beans were better than nothing.

Once we'd got our food, we began filling up one of the tables from the far end. Unfortunately, this meant that I had to sit opposite Gamble and next to Rosie Taylor. She made a massive deal out of turning her back on me. It's not like I missed out on anything, though – all she did was talk about how disgusting hot dogs were and how she was going to go on a lettuce and cress diet like this American pop-star called Eleanor Gush.

Gamble rubbed his hands together. 'This is brilliant. Free grub.'

I picked one of Mad Dan's arm hairs off my plate then stared at the chicken nuggets. Having just met their brother back at the farm, I really didn't fancy a chicken dinner at all. Even worse, though, the nuggets were absolutely burnt to a crisp from the barbeque. I *knew* this wasn't the best way to cook them! I tapped one on the table. It was so hard it made a *knock knock* noise. 'Yuck,' I said, pushing them away with my fork. At least I'd be able to eat the beans.

Or maybe not.

'Don't want your grub? Great! Can I have it then?' said Gamble, enthusiastically. The Electric Hyper had worn off and he was pretty much back to normal. Well, normal for him, at least; now he was just *extremely* excitable instead of *dangerously* excitable.

He didn't wait for an answer before shoving my chicken nuggets into his pocket and tipping my beans onto his plate. I wasn't sorry to see the back of the nuggets but I tried to ask for my beans back. Unfortunately Gamble started speaking over me and I couldn't get a word in edgeways. 'I'll save the nuggets for later but I've gotta have the beans now. I love beans, me. One time I ate three whole cans of baked beans just to see what would happen, right, and I got all this pain in my belly for ages and ages and then I just squatted down and let out the biggest f–'

At that moment, Mr Noblet sat down next to him. 'Hey, guys,' he said, plonking his plate on the table. Like me, he had chicken nuggets. 'Since Miss Clegg's helping Dan serve food, do you mind if I share your space?'

'Fine,' I squeaked. Even though Mr Noblet isn't particularly strict (apart from about the doughnuts) it's really unnerving sitting next to the headteacher, like having a policeman on your table or something.

Mr Noblet tried to push his fork into a chicken nugget but it was too hard. 'Hmmm. Thought I'd get the same as you, Roman, but they're a bit tough.'

A bit *tough?* I thought. *You could build a nuclear bunker with them.*

'You seem to have done pretty well, though,' he said, nodding towards my empty plate. I didn't feel like telling him that Gamble had cleared it for me. 'Anyway,' he continued, 'what were you saying, Darren?'

Gamble opened his mouth to finish his story.

'Nothing, sir, honest,' I said, interrupting him.

I felt the need to protect Mr Noblet here. Gamble has no shame at all and he doesn't change the way he speaks just because he's talking to an adult. I knew this because last Monday Mrs McDonald asked the class if anyone had done anything during the half-term break. Gamble stood up and said: 'I cut out pictures of bras from a catalogue.'

'Well,' said Mr Noblet, balancing the nugget on his fork and lifting it to his mouth. 'It sounded like a funny story. Don't let me stop you.'

Gamble grinned. 'Well, sir, there was this other time I had beans right and . . . '

'You've probably heard it before, sir,' I interrupted.

'No, I don't *think* I have, Roman,' said Mr Noblet. He tested the chicken nugget with his teeth then bit into it with a loud *crack*. 'Carry on, Darren.'

'Right, sir,' grinned Gamble, 'I was getting this pain in my belly, sir, and then . . . '

'Shall we talk about something else?' I said, desperately.

After crunching the chicken nugget a few times, Mr Noblet spoke with his mouth open. 'Roman, please. Let's all respect each other here.'

I put my head in my hands.

Mr Noblet carried on trying to grind up the chicken nugget. 'So you ate some beans and you were in pain,' he said. 'What happened next?'

'Well, sir . . . You'll never guess,' smiled Gamble.

'Go on.'

'I farted so hard that the dog fainted.'

Mr Noblet took a sudden intake of breath. Then he let out a strange croaking noise. A look of surprised horror flashed across his face.

I *had* tried to warn him.

'Are you alright, Mr Noblet, sir?' said Gamble.

Suddenly, Mr Noblet clutched at his throat, wheezing. His other arm swung around the table, sending his plate flying. It shattered on the concrete floor.

Mr Noblet was choking on a chicken nugget!

Was there no limit to their evilness? Now they'd started killing people!

'Hmmm,' said Gamble, 'I don't think he *is* alright, do you?'

'Course he's not alright,' I said, standing up. 'His lips are turning blue. HEEELLLLPPPP!'

Mr Noblet was now jerking about in his chair, both hands clamped round his neck. His eyes were bulging out and he was making a sound like a broken Hoover. People were pouring towards us, panicking.

'OMG! He's dying!' cried Rosie, whipping out her phone. I thought she was about to call 999 but then she announced: 'I'd better update my Facebook status.'

'Don't worry,' said Gamble, 'I know what to do. I've watched *Holby City*.'

Before I could stop him, Gamble was standing behind Mr Noblet. He grabbed our headteacher round the stomach, linking his arms at the front. Mr Noblet was twitching madly now, his face purple and terrified.

'What are you doing?' I said. Ignoring me, Gamble yanked his arms violently into Mr Noblet's stomach.

Mr Noblet's whole body jerked upwards and he made a 'FWPAAAH!' sound.

The nugget shot out of his mouth like a bullet.

Rosie screamed.

My Career's Ruined

It was totally typical of Rosie. Mr Noblet had almost died and now, five minutes later, he was drinking a glass of water with a shaky hand. Gamble had saved his life. But *she* was the one getting the most attention.

Don't get me wrong, the nugget must've whacked

her pretty hard. But she didn't have to make such a meal out of it. She'd flung herself back off her chair and was now lying on the floor, wailing and holding her eye. Her legs were waving in the air like a panicking ladybird.

Kevin 'Pukelear Missile' Harrison was kneeling by her side, cradling her head. 'Don't die,' he said, anxiously. 'I love you!'

What?! Where did that come from?

Everyone laughed like crazy.

Rosie shoved his face away. 'Get lost, barf-bag.'

I tried my best not to smile. Honestly I did. Sometimes, though, your mouth does things it's not supposed to do. Particularly when you've been having a miserable time.

Unfortunately Rosie saw me and leapt to her feet. 'Don't you dare laugh at me!' she yelled, pointing at her eye then at her neck. 'This is all your fault!'

'But . . . ' I said.

She flipped open a make-up mirror and looked at herself. Her eye was already swollen and an angry red colour. 'Look at me! What if a scout from a modelling agency turned up here tomorrow?'

'Er, why would they?' I asked.

'They're always on the look-out for beautiful girls like me,' hissed Rosie. 'You've ruined my career. You'll pay for this!'

She burst into tears.

'But I don't understand how it's my fault,' I said, genuinely confused.

'You put chicken nuggets on the menu, you brainless skid-mark,' she snapped, before spinning on her heel and storming out.

Kevin 'Pukelear Missile' Harrison begged her to wait, but she didn't stop.

Evening (and Night)

When I Had to Survive a 'Treat' from Gamble

The nugget ambush was well underway. In fact, it was starting to feel like a bombardment. Not only had I nearly drowned in wee and come face-to-face with a real-life living chicken because of them, but those bandits in breadcrumbs had now tried to kill my headteacher.

It was a code-red life-and-death situation, and it was only going to get worse.

After dinner, a couple of people (luckily not me) were asked to carry the bucket of leftovers all the way back up the hill to the wheelie bin in the car park. This made me think about my lonely doughnut at the bottom of the bin, which made me even more depressed than I already was.

While they were gone, we had twenty minutes of free time. Around the campsite, most people were talking about Kevin's declaration of love for Rosie. She was so humiliated about this, and by her black eye, that she refused to come out of her tent. I suppose this was a rare bright spot in an otherwise thoroughly miserable day.

Meanwhile, Vanya helped me put up our tent. Gamble got the hump when she told him he couldn't just prop it up using Kevin as the pole, so he sat on the grass, angrily flicking through *1001 Amazing and Disgusting Facts*.

After that, we went to our second-to-last activity of the day. On the bank of the lake we had to lay out sticks and branches to write messages for low-flying aircraft so that they could come and rescue us. I was working with Vanya but Gamble came over and gate-crashed our group. Rosie, who'd been coaxed out of her tent by Mr Noblet, sat on a log, sulking. She refused to take part in case she broke a fingernail.

Most people wrote 'S-O-S' or 'Help!' Gamble, of course, wanted us to write the word 'willy' in great big letters. Vanya said this was a bit pathetic so Gamble told her to 'go and steal someone else's best friend'. At this she just shook her head and walked off to work with someone else. I was disappointed to see her go but I could totally see her point. In fact, I'd have gone with her but Gamble would just have followed me like a piece of loo roll stuck to my welly.

When we finished, the sun was just starting to set over the lake. Mad Dan called us all together. 'People. You've survived your first day. Respect!'

He thumped his chest three times then held his fist up. Everyone cheered and did the same.

'Now. Survival ain't just about staying alive. It's about keeping your spirits up. If you let bad thoughts drag you down you're in big trouble. Do I get an kakapow?!'

Kakapow, cried the class.

Apart from me, anyway. I was thinking about all the bad things that'd happened to me that day, which were *definitely* dragging me down.

Gamble seemed to notice. 'Don't worry,' he

whispered, 'I've got that treat for you later, remember.'

'Great,' I replied. As if I wasn't feeling awful enough already.

'OK, survivors – follow me,' said Mad Dan, shouldering a huge rucksack and marching off into the woods. 'I've got something special to show you.'

We left the path and crunched through the woods until we reached a particularly tall tree. What looked like a giant bird's nest was leaning against the bottom of it. It was a kind of cone shape – about my height – with a frame of thick branches, and walls made out of sticks and leaves. 'That's my house, troops. That's where I spend every night asleep. At one with nature.'

'Do you honestly think he does live here?' murmured Vanya to me. 'I think it's all a big act.'

I smiled, delighted she was still talking to me.

We all took turns to look into the shelter through the little hole at the bottom, even though it was pretty much empty inside.

'How do you keep warm?' asked Vanya.

'If you must know, I make a quilt out of fresh leaves each night,' said Dan haughtily. 'You ask a lot of questions!'

'My Dad says you should question everything,' she replied, fixing his gaze with her eyes. Dan pursed his lips and turned away from her.

'How magical,' sighed Miss Clegg, looking at the pile of twigs and leaves like it was Buckingham Palace. 'You could leave everything behind here.'

'Where do you go to the bog?' asked Gamble, squinting at the shelter and scratching an angry zit on his neck. 'Do you dig a hole like a badger or do it out of a tree like a monkey?'

Miss Clegg glared at him, her magical moment clearly ruined.

Then Mad Dan did something *really* strange.

The Law of the Jungle

A quizzical look fell across his face. Then he reached behind his head, touched something there and let out a loud high-pitched squeak. I couldn't believe a big muscly guy could make a noise like that! Honestly, it sounded like someone had strangled a mole.

'What's wrong?' exclaimed Miss Clegg, looking concerned.

Mad Dan leapt up into her arms, clutching her

neck with one hand like a baby. She looked delighted. Dan slapped at the back of his neck with his other hand. 'Getitoffmegetitoffme!' he shrieked, his eyes wild with terror.

Calmly, Gamble stepped forward and pulled something off the back of Mad Dan's neck. 'Oooh, look. A spider,' he grinned, tilting his head back and dangling the poor little thing above his open mouth by a strand of its silk. I swear he was about to eat it before Vanya made him let it go.

Once the spider had scuttled off across the forest floor, everyone's attention very slowly turned back to our instructor. He had lowered himself out of Miss Clegg's arms, but his face was bright red.

'Scared of an incy-wincy spider?' said Vanya, half-mocking him. 'I thought you were a survival expert?'

She had a point there.

'You can die of spider bites,' said Dan, taking deep breaths and trying to regain his calm. 'I've had to suck spider poison out of my own toes in the jungle before. I'm not scared. Just . . . cautious. Who'd look after you if I wasn't here?'

'You looked pretty scared to me,' said Vanya, trying not to laugh.

Without replying, Mad Dan ground his teeth together and stomped off again. Miss Clegg rushed up alongside him to check he was OK.

'I'm telling you, there's something weird about Mad Dan,' said Vanya, watching him disappear into the woods. 'And I'm going to find out what.'

Camp Fire

We'd been trailing after Dan and Miss Clegg for ages when we eventually came to a clearing in the woods. A large pentagon of tree trunks had been laid on the ground. In the centre was a pyramid of sticks and branches, about one and a half times the height of Mad Dan. There was a faint smell of that flammable stuff my dad squirts onto the barbeque in the summer. We all sat down on the logs and Mad Dan stood in the middle, removing his rucksack and dropping it behind him.

'Bosh,' he announced, striking a match and holding it up in the air. He seemed back to his normal self again. 'We're gonna have us an old-fashioned campfire.'

He flicked the match onto the bottom of the sticks. There was a *woof* noise, and flames began to lick up into the air. Everyone went *Oooooh*.

'Make sure Darren doesn't get too close,' said Mr Noblet, leaning into Miss Clegg's ear.

Miss Clegg didn't look happy about this. 'Can't we just tie him to a tree?' she moaned.

I think she wanted to sit next to Mad Dan.

The campfire wasn't all that bad, though. We sang some silly songs. Most of the words were nonsense like 'unga bunga wunga, dance like a caveman' or 'who's seen my cheese? It's there behind your knees. Who's seen my stickers? They're in your granny's knickers' and so on, but they took my mind off things for a while at least.

The evening took a bit of a turn for the worse when Dan pulled a guitar from behind a nearby tree and crooned one of his own songs. Everybody linked arms and swayed from side to side but I thought it was completely lame. His voice was whiny and scratchy, and the song was all about how he wanted to 'dance through the treetops with a natural woman'.

When he sang this last bit, Miss Clegg almost fell off her log.

In fact, she was so enchanted that Darren was able to slip away for five minutes, but I think I was the only one who noticed.

'Where have you been?' she asked when he got back. After an undeserved round of applause, Dan had thankfully now put his guitar away.

Gamble turned out his pockets and plopped down in his seat. 'I ain't nicked nothing, you can't prove it, I'm innocent.'

'Sorry, dudes,' said Dan, poking round the big rucksack. 'Thought I'd brought three bags of marshmallows but I've only got two. Never mind – should still be enough for one each.'

For some reason, Gamble looked up into the sky and started whistling.

Marshmallows

As the flames died down a bit, Mad Dan handed round wooden skewers to everyone (apart from Gamble who isn't allowed sharp things), then passed around marshmallows for us to toast. This was pretty exciting. I mean, obviously they're no match for a doughnut, but I hadn't eaten anything since breakfast and they were definitely better than nuggets. At last, something sweet!

I was just about to stab my skewer through the marshmallow when Rosie called out, 'Hey! You can't let Roman have one. It's against his diet.'

As if to make absolutely certain, she pulled the marshmallow off my stick and flung it into the fire. I watched as it sizzled and turned black.

I no longer had the strength to argue.

'OK,' announced Mad Dan, as everyone else slurped their marshmallows and made *mnyam mnyam* noises. 'Whenever you're in a survival situation, it's important to have a leader. So each day at the campfire we're gonna choose someone to be tribal chief. The chief gets to make one rule that the rest of us have got to follow until a new chief is elected.'

This would've sounded quite cool. If I'd had any chance of winning, that is.

Before we voted, we nominated the people who we thought deserved to be tribal chief. Mr Noblet chose Gamble, because he'd saved his life at dinner time. Kevin nominated Rosie Taylor, which made everybody else howl with laughter. And Miss Clegg suggested Vanya. She didn't explain why but I guessed it was because Vanya had beaten up Gamble on the bus.

Then we had to put our hands up to vote. Gamble got two votes (one from Mr Noblet and one from me because he told me he'd chuck me in the fire if I didn't), Rosie also got one vote (from Kevin), Mad Dan got one vote (from Miss Clegg) even though he wasn't nominated. Everyone else voted for Vanya.

Rosie was furious and screamed that the whole class was jealous of how beautiful she was, before storming back to her tent with Kevin gazing after her.

'What's your rule going to be?' said Mad Dan, plonking a feathery Native American headdress on Vanya's head. To be honest he also seemed a bit annoyed that she'd won it.

Vanya thought for a moment. 'I think Roman should be allowed a marshmallow,' she said. 'It's not fair that he didn't get one.'

Wow! What an amazing friend. I could've wept. 'Thank you so much,' I croaked.

Vanya shrugged. 'What are friends for?'

'I'm not sure he's allowed . . . ' said Mr Noblet uneasily.

'That's a good point,' said Mad Dan, who still seemed miffed with me about the sick on his car and the water zorb. 'You'll have to come up with something else.'

Vanya frowned. 'No. I'm the chief and you said I could make a rule. Everyone heard you.' There was a steeliness to her voice like she wasn't going to back down. 'It's either that or I make a rule that you've got to sit in a bath of spiders . . . '

Mad Dan shivered. And so I was allowed to eat a beautifully-toasted, crispy, gooey marshmallow. It was incredible, sliding down my throat in a wave of sweet stickiness. I sat there for ages afterwards, scraping the last of it off the skewer with my teeth. Obviously it wasn't as good as a doughnut but still, it was definitely better than a paper-cut to the eyeball.

The moment was finally ruined when Gamble came over and burped in my ear. 'That's nothing,' he whispered.

'What's nothing?' I replied.

He nodded towards the stick. 'That treat Vanya gave you. I've still not given you mine yet. Wait til everyone else is asleep later. You'll see what your real best mate's got for you.'

I gulped, then threw the stick onto the fire and watched it slowly burn away.

My 'Treat'

Back at the tent I climbed inside my sleeping bag and tried to get to sleep. This was impossible for three reasons. First, we'd been given inflatable mattresses but they were so thin I could feel the stones on the ground underneath digging into my ribs. Second, Kevin was snoring like a tortured buffalo. And third – Gamble.

He lay sprawled across the tent, still in his stinky clothes, with his dirty dog-flannel rolled up as a pillow. And he just. Would. Not. Shut. Up.

'Do you want your treat now, Roman?'

'I think I'll get some sleep.'

'Suit yourself.'

Three second pause.

'What about now?'

'Still no.'

Two second pause.

'Now?'

'. . .'

One second pause.

'How about now?'

I sat up. 'If I say yes, will you let me go to sleep?'

'Course,' said Gamble, flicking on his torch and shining it under his chin so that creepy shadows were cast across his face. 'You're gonna love this.'

He was *so* wrong about that.

Holding the torch in his mouth, he rummaged around in his plastic bag. Eventually he pulled out a sewing needle and two small metal rings and held them up like they were precious jewels. 'Ta-da! Your treat, best mate.'

I looked at them uneasily. 'Why have you brough–'

'Me and you are getting matching piercings,' interrupted Gamble. He was so excited he was pretty much bouncing up and down. 'You stab the needle through your ear then quickly put the earring in before it's got time to heal. If we do it now the scabs'll drop off by the time we get home.'

'*That* was the treat you've been on about all day?' I said, shuffling away from him.

'Course!' said Gamble. 'What could be better than two best mates who look the same? I'll shave your head as well if you like.'

I tried to ignore this last bit. 'But wouldn't it . . . hurt?'

'Don't be soft!' he exclaimed. 'My brother Spud did it for him and Scratchy and neither of 'em cried about it.'

Only Gamble could have a pet dog with pierced ears.

Somewhere in the distance an owl hooted. 'But Darren, I don't want my ears pierced.'

Gamble sniffed. 'Fair enough.'

'What . . . *really*?' I said. Normally Gamble doesn't take no for an answer.

'Yeah,' he replied. 'Pull up your pyjama top. We'll have matching belly-button rings instead.'

I put a protective hand over my stomach. 'I don't want my belly button done either.'

'Fine,' said Gamble, exasperated. 'Nipples it is.'

Yikes.

I rubbed my eyes and gave a deep sigh. 'Look, I don't want to be pierced. I'm tired. I'm hungry. I thought when you said you had a treat that it might be, you know, *food*.'

Gamble thought about this for a moment. 'How about a chicken nugget?'

He cheerfully handed me one from his pocket.

It was warm but I wasn't sure whether this was from the barbeque or from him. I sniffed it and instantly recoiled. The nugget smelled exactly like Gamble, only five times stronger. Imagine a six-day-old dead pigeon stuffed with old pants and burnt hair, and you'd be pretty close.

'I don't think I want it,' I said.

'Why not?' said Gamble, accusingly. 'What's wrong with it? Don't you want to be my mate any more?'

I gulped. 'I mean, I don't want it *now*. I'll save it for later,' I said, placing it on the groundsheet as far away from my nose as I could.

'Awesome!' said Gamble. 'Hey! Remember when Dan said he thought he'd brought an extra bag of marshmallows?'

Up until that moment I'd forgotten about this, but I nodded my head anyway.

'He had.'

A tickly feeling gathered in my stomach. 'How do you know, Darren?'

'The other one's up a tree. I nicked it earlier and hid it when he was singing that rubbish song.'

I sat bolt upright.

Gamble grinned at me proudly. 'Fancy a little stroll through the woods?'

Sneaking About

Now, before I carry on, I will say that I know that what we did was wrong. But because of the chicken nugget diet, I was seriously hungry and craving something sweet. Clearly, marshmallows wouldn't be my first-choice snack, but the thought of stuffing my face with them was enough to make me break a few rules. Plus, I had a taste for them now.

We slipped out of the tent and tip-toed from shadow to shadow across the campsite, avoiding the dim light of the lamps that were dotted around and half-expecting to be caught at any moment. We had to be extra quiet when we crept past Mr Noblet's tent (which had a light on inside) and Miss Clegg's (which didn't). My heart was thumping as we finally reached the pitch darkness of the woods.

We could hear the cows at the farm mooing as they settled down for the night. The cool air and anticipation made me shiver. I didn't want to admit it, but this was great fun.

Gamble had brought his torch, but even so the woods were pretty spooky. There were shadows and brambles and branches that jabbed you as you walked past. Occasionally something would rustle or hoot.

Or talk.

'Sssh!' I said, pulling Gamble behind a tree trunk. 'Who's that?'

We switched off the torch and peeped round the tree. About ten metres away, Miss Clegg and Mad Dan were sitting next to each other by the dying embers of the fire. *What were they doing here*?

'I hid the marshmallows right above their heads,' whispered Gamble. 'I'll go get 'em.'

'No, stop!' I hissed, grabbing his arm. 'We'll get in massive trouble.'

I was starting to think that this was a seriously bad idea.

Because the woods were so quiet, we could hear everything Miss Clegg and Dan were saying. I felt bad listening to them but I couldn't really help it. Well, I could've done but once I'd started I couldn't stop myself. It was like when you have a box of doughnuts and you eat the first one. You know you shouldn't eat the other eleven in one go . . . but you do.

Well, *I* do anyway.

Their conversation went like this:

Miss Clegg:	He's just awful. I've got to spend every day with him. It's like having a disease.
Mad Dan:	Sounds like he totally drags you down and crushes your spirit.
Miss Clegg:	He does. A couple of weeks ago we went to an aquarium. I was honestly hoping he'd get eaten by a squid.

At this point Gamble looked at me with a big goofy grin on his face, and whispered, 'Whoever she's talking about sounds like a right idiot.'

I forced a smile back. He clearly didn't realise Miss Clegg was talking about him. The conversation continued:

Mad Dan:	So quit your job. Leave it all behind. Be free.
Miss Clegg:	I wish I could.
Mad Dan:	You could. You're a beautiful soul.
Miss Clegg:	Hey! I could come here and work for you.

Mad Dan:	Ah. Well. I mean. I'd have to ask . . .
Miss Clegg:	It'd be perfect. I could be your assistant and hel— [*She suddenly farts loudly*]
Mad Dan:	What was *that*?
Miss Clegg:	Er . . . *ahem*. I think it was an owl.

This was too much for Gamble. 'Haha! Nice pump, miss!' he cried, leaping out from behind the tree.

By the time Miss Clegg and Mad Dan had turned round and called out, we were already sprinting away.

Sleep When You're Dead

Two minutes later, Gamble and I were bent double in our tent, catching our breath.

'That was hilarious!' panted Gamble. 'What do you wanna do next?'

'She's going to murder us,' I said, pulling brambles out of my jumper. My skin had been completely shredded from running through the woods. 'I'm going to bed.'

'You can sleep when you're dead,' said Gamble, twitching excitedly. 'Let's go chuck stuff off the climbing wall!'

'Definitely not,' I replied, climbing back into my sleeping bag.

'Aw, don't be like that,' he said. 'I'll get you something brilliant. I promise.'

I said nothing.

'Wait 'til you see what I pinch for you! It'll blow your socks off!'

Gamble's voice sounded desperate now but I still didn't bother to turn around. What would've been the point? The marshmallows were off-limits. There was a long pause, then the tent zip went up and down again, and he was gone.

As I settled down to sleep, I started to think about what Miss Clegg had said. No wonder she was thinking about getting another job. Gamble *was* like a disease. Except instead of making me ill he just got me into trouble. Plus, he didn't seem to know what was going on around him – I mean, he never realised when he was being a pain. I was definitely better off without him.

But then again, part of me felt really guilty for letting him go out on his own. You could never tell what he might do next. *Wait 'til you see what I pinch for you!* What did he mean by that? I imagined him crawling down a hole and being savaged by angry rabbits, or climbing up a tree to try to catch a bat for me. He could plummet down and . . .

Good grief. What had I done?

And so I couldn't sleep at all. I sat up in my bed, waiting. The only sound was Kevin snoring loudly. *Honk . . . Shoooo . . . Honk . . . Shoooo . . .* Occasionally he would mumble Rosie's name, which was really horrible – he'd even started dreaming about her.

Time dragged on. How long had Gamble been gone for? Lying there in the dark, I started counting the snores. I got up to one thousand, two hundred and thirty-six, becoming more and more worried with each one. I was genuinely thinking of going to wake up Mr Noblet when the zip finally opened again.

'Darren?' I said, blinking against the darkness. 'Is that you?'

Gamble switched on his torch and shone it in my eyes. 'Splash down!' he cried, before diving up in the air and landing flat on top of me.

'Ow!' I shouted, my voice muffled by Gamble's body. I shoved him off. The tent went dark as

Gamble's torch bounced away. I fought my way to my feet and found the torch, which had landed on Kevin's pillow. He'd slept through the whole thing and was now cuddling the torch and muttering something about how beautiful Rosie was. *Yuck!* I slipped it out of his grasp and shone the light onto Gamble, who was lying on top of my crumpled sleeping bag, laughing his head off.

'Awesome!' he howled.

'No, it's not "awesome",' I snapped. 'What did you do that for?'

Gamble stopped laughing and sat up. 'I just wanted to wake you up 'cos I went to the kitchen, right, and it was unlocked, right, so I nicked you your favourite food, innit.'

I felt my belly grumble. 'What? You mean . . . a doughnut?'

'Even better,' he replied, sounding worryingly pleased with himself. 'Look over there.'

Even better than doughnuts? It wasn't possible. Unless he'd stolen a doughnut with another doughnut inside it.

Nervously excited, I flashed the torch over. There was an enormous plastic sack, bigger than a pillow, sitting next to the zip.

Questions went fizzing through my brain. How had Gamble carried that great big sack back here? How had he managed to nick it? And most importantly, **what exactly was inside it?**

I shone the torch to get a closer look and instantly felt my whole body sag. 'Darren,' I said, trying to keep my voice steady, 'why have you stolen two hundred frozen chicken nuggets?'

'Well . . . durrr,' said Gamble. 'I told you. They're your favourites.'

I closed my eyes and pinched the bridge of my nose. 'No, they aren't.'

'But you're always eating them,' he replied, his voice wobbling. 'I had to break into the big freezer in the kitchens and everything. I tried to carry three bags but they were too heavy so I left the other two behind. I'll get them later if you li–'

I dropped to my knees. 'I *hate* them!!' I cried. 'I hate them more than anything in the whole world. Not only are they disgusting but they're ruining my flipping life!'

'So . . . ' said Gamble, sounding deeply confused, 'you don't want to eat them, then?'

'Of course not!' I shouted. 'And in any case,

they're *frozen.* How are we going to cook them?'

Gamble thought for a minute. 'Well, there was this thing in my fact book about a man in New Zealand who cooks things in his armpit and . . . '

'You and your stupid fact book,' I growled.

'We could shove a stick in them. They'd be just like ice lollies.'

At this point I was about to tell Gamble that I'd shove a stick in him if he didn't get rid of the chicken nuggets but there was a sound of someone clearing their throat from the outside of the tent. My whole body turned to stone.

'Everything alright in there?' came Mr Noblet's sleepy voice from the other side.

'Yes, sir, I was just having a *nightmare*,' I replied, staring directly at Gamble. 'But I'll be fine.'

Mr Noblet mumbled something. There was the sound of retreating footsteps rustling through the grass outside.

I dropped my voice to an angry hiss. 'Why do you have to destroy *everything*? Just take them away.'

Gamble leapt to his feet and waggled his finger in my face. 'No,' he said, defiantly. 'I'm trying to be a good friend and you're just . . . *mean*. All I wanted was to be your friend. And you keep leaving me for that stupid girl Vanya.'

'But . . . but . . . ' I said. 'Hang on. Are you *jealous* of her?'

'No,' sulked Gamble.

I suddenly felt really, really bad. No wonder he'd been playing up all day. I mean, I know Gamble is totally nuts, and naughty and a little bit, well, *scuzzy*, but he *is* supposed to be my best friend after all. And he seemed genuinely disappointed that I didn't want this sack of frozen nuggets.

'Look,' I sighed, 'I'll work with you tomorrow, OK. I promise.'

Gamble instantly cheered up. 'Brilliant!' he exclaimed, before flopping down onto the ground to go to sleep.

I was in a very dangerous position. I was surrounded by chicken nuggets and they were destroying my life in two different ways; there were the obvious catastrophes like my new diet, Mad Dan's car and the zorb. But they were also destroying my life more slowly and subtly at the same time. I mean, the nuggets had helped me gain a new friend in Vanya, but this in turn had made Gamble jealous and more determined than ever to win my friendship. And trust me, this was not a good thing.

TUESDAY

Morning

When I Survived Being Lost and Caught in a Flap

Breakfast was terrible. Down at the canteen, Mad Dan stood in front of us all. 'Awooga, survivors! Who slept well?'

Most people grumbled and groaned in response. Rosie Taylor was slumped face down on a table, enormous black glasses covering her eyes.

'I smashed a great night's sleep in my shelter,' Dan said. 'Just the bats and the owls for company.'

'Amazing,' sighed Miss Clegg.

'Where do you keep your clothes?' asked Vanya. 'They look really clean and well-ironed.'

She was right about this. His skin-tight polo shirt was completely immaculate.

Mad Dan went a little bit red. He cleared his throat and attempted to ignore her. 'Moving on . . .' he said. 'Somehow two bags of chicken nuggets were left out of the freezer last night . . . '

Gamble inspected his shoes really closely.

'So,' continued Mad Dan, 'I'm afraid you'll all have to have them for breakfast before they go off.'

Awwwww! said everyone.

'That's survival,' said Mad Dan. 'You do what needs to be done.'

'What will you be eating?' asked Vanya.

'I feasted on nuts and berries from the forest floor this morning,' replied Dan.

Vanya twisted up her mouth. 'That's funny. I went down to the games pitch to practise karate this morning and I swear I saw your car parked outside the farmhouse.'

Miss Clegg glared at her.

Mad Dan ground his teeth together. 'I had business to take care of.'

'Like eating breakfast, perhaps?' she said, trying to keep her face as innocent as possible.

He muttered something under his breath, before angrily serving up the chicken nuggets.

'Oi,' hissed Gamble to Vanya. 'Why do you keep having a go at Mad Dan, you big crusty nose wipe?'

'My dad says you should always question stuff,' shrugged Vanya. 'Mad Dan reckons he lives in the wild and I don't believe him, that's all.'

'Dunno why you wanna be mates with her,' said Gamble to me, standing up to go and collect his nuggets. 'She's proper mental.'

Toddler Tantrum

During breakfast I managed to force down three nuggets. Gamble ate about fifteen and put another three in his pocket. Most other people reluctantly nibbled a couple with their toast. Rosie Taylor didn't move, her head rested on folded arms.

After we'd all finished eating, Mr Noblet tapped her on the shoulder and asked if she'd mind slopping out the leftovers today.

Rosie forced her head up and removed her sunglasses. Her black eye was enormous and she looked terrible – all pale and blotchy. 'Yes, I would mind,' she whispered hoarsely. 'Get these atrocious rejects to do it.' She waved a hand at me, Vanya and Gamble.

'But everyone has to take a turn,' pleaded Mr Noblet.

'I've told you,' growled Rosie, getting steadily more annoyed, 'I've not slept a wink and I'm not doing it.'

'It's only a little job,' said Mr Noblet gently. 'Kevin Harrison can help you.'

Everyone went insane at this, bouncing around like baboons.

'Definitely!' said Kevin 'Pukelear Missile' Harrison, leaping excitedly to his feet.

This only made Rosie more angry. 'Urgh. Yucktabulous,' she snarled. 'I'd honestly rather sandpaper my tongue.'

'Now now,' said Mr Noblet, 'I know you're upset but let's value our classmates here.'

Rosie was having none of it, though. She was winding herself up into a full-on toddler tantrum. 'I've got a black eye. A bruised neck. My hair looks like a bird's been living in it. My modelling career will be in tatters. This morning there was a mouse in my shower. A *mouse*! I'm having a mental breakdown here and all you care about is making me carry half-chewed food up a hill with the Grand Old Puke of York. Well, you can stick your stupid residential!'

With that she burst into tears and stormed off out of the canteen and back towards her tent.

There was a mix of reactions from the group. Gamble thought it was 'well-mega-wicked' but most people looked shocked, or even like they felt sorry for her. A couple of girls ran after Rosie to make sure she was OK. Of course I thought she was over-reacting.

Kevin was sitting alone on a bench. 'She called me the Grand Old Puke of York,' he said, sadly.

I patted him on the shoulder. As much as I dislike Rosie, I have to say this *was* a pretty awesome new nickname for him.

I had to say something a bit nicer than this, though. 'Have you ever thought about fancying someone else?' *You know, someone who's* not *a total idiot?*

'No, she's perfect,' he said, staring into my eyes. 'What can I do to make her like me, Roman?'

'Er . . . I'm not sure,' I said. *Change absolutely everything about yourself, perhaps?* What I couldn't understand was this: why would Kevin want Rosie to like him? She was so evil!

Mad Dan clapped his hands together. He didn't seem to have any time for sympathy towards Rosie or Kevin. 'Like I've said before – only the strongest will survive. Let's hustle.'

Extreme Orienteering

Ten minutes later, we were all standing somewhere in the middle of the woods. Mad Dan stood on top of a tree stump, looking down on us. 'Awooga, dudes!' he announced, flexing his biceps. 'Give me a *yippy-kai-yay* if you're ready for some extreme three-legged orienteering.'

Everyone cried *yippy-kai-yay*!

'You've gotta find your way round the woods in pairs,' he continued, waving his huge, muscly arm to demonstrate the space. 'But there's a catch. Survivors have to face incredible challenges . . . So each group's gotta tie their ankles together.'

People looked at their partners, giggling.

'Wicked,' said Gamble, putting his arm round my shoulder. Of course Gamble hadn't let me forget my promise to work with him.

'So, dudes,' announced Dan after we'd had our ankles tied together, 'hit the woods. Find the points marked on your maps and collect the letters from each point to make a word.'

'Who are you going to be tied to, Dan?' said Miss Clegg.

'I'll stay here, I think . . . ' he replied.

'Me too,' said Miss Clegg quickly. She looked like she'd just found a packet of Rolos down the back of her sofa.

Mr Noblet leaned towards her and coughed. 'Er, Miss Clegg. Are you sure you shouldn't be with Darr–' he began, but she interrupted him.

'He'll be fine,' she said, folding her arms. 'And maybe this afternoon you and I can have a chat about my future.'

Mr Noblet looked confused.

'I've had an interesting offer,' she said, glancing knowingly at Mad Dan.

'But . . . '

'Not now,' replied Miss Clegg. 'Later.'

Just then Dan shouted 'Go!' and the other groups scattered in different directions, carefully moving their legs at the same time. I was looking at the map to see where the closest point was when

Gamble yelled, 'This way!' and started sprinting, dragging me in his wake.

I don't know if you've ever tried moving around while tied to another person but it's *really* difficult. You've got to step in perfect time with each other. If one person decides to run off you've got a choice – do your best to follow them and stay on your feet, or don't and fall over. I hit the deck several times before realising that I should just accept that I was being led by Gamble. I was sort of hoping he would tire himself out.

Five minutes later, we were completely lost. Gamble had pulled me through the woods, across the driveway, through some more woods, over a broken barbed-wire fence and through a load of thick bushes. We were now standing by the bank of a steep ditch, looking down on the stream that was running along the bottom of it. In the distance, we could hear other kids from our class shouting and laughing.

'Hmmm,' said Gamble. 'Should we have a look at the map?'

'Little bit late for that,' I replied flatly. 'We went off the edge of the map ages ago. We should just go back and –'

'No!' snapped Gamble. 'A Gamble never goes back. I reckon we keep going and we'll find one of the points sooner or later.'

I shook my head. 'Not unless we walk all the way round the world. The points are all behind us.'

'Hey!' he said. 'I've got an idea.'

He pulled the sewing needle out of his pocket.

'I told you last night,' I said. 'You aren't piercing any part of my body.'

'Don't worry, best mate. I'm gonna wait 'til you're asleep for that,' he said, matter-of-factly. He rummaged about in his other pocket, removed one of the chicken nuggets from breakfast and held it up proudly in the air. 'I've got a better idea.'

'You're going to give a chicken nugget an earring?' I said. 'Have you gone totally mad?'

'Er . . . no,' he said, shaking his head. 'Don't you remember that fact from my book?'

I remembered him droning on and on by the tent yesterday. 'You mean the one about that orang-utan who learned to play the piano?'

Gamble rolled his eyes. 'No. The one about the man who escaped from the desert by making a compass out of a needle, a fridge magnet and a dead lizard's eyeball.'

'A compass?' I said.

'It's a thing that helps you find North.'

'I know what a compass is but we don't *need* to find North,' I said. 'We just need to go back the way we c–'

'Rubbish,' interrupted Gamble. 'Anyway, chicken nuggets probably have some eyeball in 'em.'

'Don't tell me that,' I said. 'I've been eating them all week.'

Gamble ignored me. 'So, we shove the needle through the nugget, float it in some water and it'll turn round to face North. Then we go from there. Survival skills, innit?'

Although I had to admit this was actually good thinking, it had to be the most ridiculous idea I'd ever heard in my entire life. 'Number one,' I said, 'we're not in the desert. Number two, we're about four hundred metres from where we started. And number three, it's pointless; if we just turned around we'd get back there in no time.'

Without answering, Gamble yanked his leg forward, flipping me onto my backside and causing both of us to slide down the ditch. 'Let's do this,' he said, when our feet splashed into the stream at the bottom.

Gamble Finds the Way

After sticking the needle through the chicken nugget, Gamble plopped it into the stream. It bobbed up and down a few times before floating away in the fast-flowing water. We watched it disappear into a drainage pipe.

'That must be North then,' he said triumphantly.

'I think you're meant to do it in *still* water,' I replied, pulling off a sharp bramble that was stuck into my buttock. 'And I think you have to rub the needle with a magnet first or something.'

'Right, well, we'll go East, which is over there,' he said, ignoring me and pointing his finger in a completely random direction.

'But Darren, if we go that way we'll end up in the farmer's field. Remember what Dan said – if we go in there *bad things will happen*.'

'Like what?' he snorted.

'You know. Stuff.'

I felt too embarrassed to mention the creepy chicken.

Gamble started clambering up the other side of the ditch. Still tied to his ankle, I hopped up and down a few times before being forced to follow him.

It's really difficult to make your own decisions when you're tied to someone else, particularly when that person is a total maniac. At the top of the slope, we reached a wooden fence. I was about to ask what we were going to do next when Gamble suddenly swung his free leg over it then did the same with his other one, jerking my foot up and flipping me over. I was now upside down with one leg over the fence and Gamble trying to tug the rest of my body after it.

After about two minutes of being dangled around like a fish on a hook, he finally managed to haul me over onto the other side of the fence.

'Right, that's it! I've had enough,' I said, untying the rope from my ankle.

We found ourselves about halfway along a large field. There was a single cow in the corner, munching grass and staring hard at us. Further down, there was a second field with more cows in it. Beyond that was the empty field I'd rescued the ball from yesterday, with the barns and farmhouse alongside it.

'Look,' I said wearily, 'if we head down there we can at least get back into the games pitch.'

Gamble wasn't listening, though. His eyes had drifted towards something over my shoulder. Gamble's always doing this. Honestly, there are maggots with better concentration spans than him.

'What now?' I sighed.

Gamble screwed up his face. 'What's that cow's problem? It's proper staring at us.'

'It's probably never seen anyone quite like you before,' I replied.

'There was a fact in my book about cows,' said Gamble. 'You can lead one upstairs but . . . hmmm, how did it end again?'

I glanced over at the cow and frowned. There was something a little bit strange about it. Its eyes were yellow and it was glaring right at us. 'Maybe we should get out of the field,' I said. 'It doesn't look like it wants us here . . . '

Gamble sniffed. 'Do you think it's on its own 'cos it doesn't have any mates?'

'What are you talking about?'

'They probably pick on it 'cos it doesn't have boobs.'

'"Boobs"? What are you on about?'

'The ones in the other field have got boobs. This one ain't. Maybe they bully her. That's why she got her nose pierced. To show 'em she's hard so they don't mess with her.'

I gulped. I'd just realised what was strange about the cow. Gamble was right. It had no udders. And it had a ring through its nose. And it was twice as big as the ones in the other field. And, worst of all, it was slowly wandering towards us.

'That's not a cow,' I said, my voice shaking. 'It's a . . . BULL!'

The bull flung its massive head back and stamped on the ground a few times. It was about the size of a car and it had two enormous, sharp horns. I took a step backwards. Everyone knows you don't mess with bulls. Still glaring with its yellow eyes, it broke into a steady trot.

'A bull?' said Gamble. 'Ace!'

'No. Not ace,' I shouted, pulling him back by his arm. 'Very, very *not* ace. Let's go.'

I tried to drag him away but Gamble stayed still. Before I could stop him, he'd whipped off his t-shirt.

'What are you doing, you nutter?' I cried.

'Bull-fighting, innit,' he grinned, holding his

t-shirt in the air and flapping it up and down. His skinny little body shone in the sun. 'Come on, bull. What've you got?'

The bull stopped and gave a huge snotty huff.

Then it lowered its head and charged right at us.

I screamed and absolutely legged it towards the next field. Behind me the thundering footsteps got closer and closer. I reached the fence and flung myself over, landing painfully on the other side.

But what about Gamble?

I span round to look. He hadn't followed me! What was he thinking? He'd somehow dodged the bull's first attack. Now he was beckoning it towards him with his free hand and shouting, 'Let's have it, then!'

The bull ran at him again. I could barely watch. This was going to be awful.

Then, at the very last moment, Gamble whipped his t-shirt up in the air and leapt out of the way. The t-shirt got tangled up on the bull's horns and it blundered around, blindly flinging its head from side to side.

'Woo-hooo!' screamed Gamble.

'Get out of there!' I yelled.

'Calm down, Dad,' called Gamble. 'This is amazing!'

He slapped the bull on the backside and, as it span round, he pulled his t-shirt off its horns. Then he decided to pull a moony at it, which sent the bull absolutely mental. Gamble howled with laughter and ran towards me, pulling up his trousers and zig-zagging out of the way of the bull's horns. Just as it was about to spear him, he dived forward and rolled under the fence, lying topless in the grass and laughing hysterically.

Behind us, the bull skidded to a halt millimetres from the fence. It snorted and tossed its head, staring at us murderously before turning around and trudging angrily away.

'Phew! How much fun was that?' Gamble exclaimed, standing up to face me, brushing dried grass off his clothes. 'We're safe, eh, mate?'

'Are you insane?' I said.

Gamble looked confused. 'Just having a laugh, innit?'

'No wonder Miss Clegg wants to get away from you,' I said, turning around and storming off.

'What's that supposed to mean?' called Gamble behind me.

Fuming, I span round to face him. 'Haven't you listened to her? She's getting another job because she's fed . . . '

'Hey!' cried a man's voice from across the field.

We both looked over. A short, red-faced man with bandy legs was marching towards us. I guessed he was the farmer because he was wearing overalls and wellies and . . . *Holy nuggets!* He had a shotgun over his arm.

'What are you two doing with that bull?' he roared.

'Let's get out of here!' cried Gamble. 'He's packing heat!'

Heart pounding, I followed Gamble as he legged it across the field, past the herd of cows, through a gate and into the courtyard between the farmhouse and the barns.

'In here!' Gamble said, opening a door and dragging me into one of the barns.

We slammed the door behind us and ducked behind a bale of hay.

'Phew! That was close,' panted Gamble. 'That farmer looked like he wanted to ice us.'

I didn't answer.

I'd just seen what was in the barn.

The Worst Nightmare Possible. Times a Million

Imagine the worst nightmare you possibly can. Then times it by a million. Let me guess what you thought of:

You're buried alive in a coffin along with someone who's got diarrhoea.

What I saw was worse than that.

You're standing in front of the whole school completely nude.

What I saw was worse than that.

Your *headteacher* is standing in front of the whole school completely nude.

OK. What I saw was not *quite* worse than that. But still . . . it was really, really bad.

We were standing in a huge barn – easily three times the size of our school hall. And every square centimetre of space was completely filled.

With chickens.

Chickens.

Seriously. There were *millions* of them, stretching off into the distance like a big, rippling feathery carpet. The smell burnt my throat and nose and made my eyes stream. I backed away towards the wall, nearly tripping over the hay bale.

It seemed like every single one of their beady black eyes was staring at us. Here and there, heads were tilted, feathers were ruffled, wings flapped uselessly. These individual movements gave the impression of small waves on an otherwise calm, brown sea. The only noise was a constant muttering of *bwark bwark bwark*.

'We need to get out of here,' I whispered, trying desperately to keep the panic out of my voice.

From outside the barn we could hear footsteps in the courtyard. The farmer with the shotgun was wandering about. We couldn't go that way. The closest other door was halfway down the long side of the barn.

We were going to have to walk through the chickens.

Very slowly, and holding my nose, I edged through the barn. The first few chickens parted for me, pecking at the ground around my wellies. *OK*, I thought, my heart hammering and my breath coming in shallow rasps, *easy does it. Nice and slow. Maybe this isn't as bad as . . .*

Of course, I hadn't considered Gamble.

'Hey, Roman!' he said, way too loudly. 'Do you think they know I've got chicken nuggets in my pocket?'

There was a quick flurry of wings. A couple of chickens half-flew in front of me. I stood completely still.

'Ssssshh,' I hissed angrily. The chickens slowly settled down and I edged forwards again.

'I mean,' boomed Gamble, louder than before, 'this could be their brother! Hey – watch this . . .'

Now I'm not saying that the chickens *knew* what was in the nugget. I mean, maybe it was Gamble's sudden movement that caused them to panic, as he sprinted across the barn and leapt onto a hay bale, screaming: 'Save yourselves, chickens! Don't get turned into one of these!'

Or perhaps it was because the farmer suddenly came through the door and yelled: 'Come out of there!'

The reason why is unimportant. What *is* important is that the barn suddenly exploded into a full-on flap-fest.

It was chaos.

Within seconds, the air was a whirlwind of panicking birds, beating wings, flying dust, angry beaks and flashing talons. I found myself knocked to the ground, choking and blinded by this surging storm of birds. They stampeded across my face. They pecked and scratched me. They smacked into the side of my head. Little splats of nasty white stuff flew everywhere.

Somewhere ahead, Gamble seemed to be swallowed up by the seething mass of poultry. 'Darren!' I cried, but he was gone.

Somehow I struggled to my feet and blindly stumbled across the barn, tripping and wheezing and flailing my arms around. Ahead of me was a rectangle of light. Somehow the door was open! I staggered towards it, chickens crashing into me from all angles, until finally I got outside, spitting out a mouthful of feathers and gulping the fresh air. My clothes were torn to shreds and my skin felt like I'd slid down a giant cheese-grater. Blood seeped out of a thousand tiny cuts all over my body and I felt seriously faint.

Above my head, a powerful river of chickens hurtled out to freedom. More and more flew out, like bats from a cave, landing then zipping along the grass with rapid little steps. The cows in the field stared at them indifferently. I tried to see where they were going but I was dizzy and my vision was blurred.

From the barn, the farmer came blundering outside with his arms outstretched. Thankfully he no longer had his shotgun. 'Come back!' he yelled.

Unsurprisingly, the chickens ignored him.

'I'm not an expert but I don't think they're very good at following instructions,' I said. At the time I thought I was being helpful but my voice was all slurred and it sounded like someone else was talking.

The farmer turned to face me but I couldn't focus. It felt like I was spinning round on a roundabout. 'Excuse me, I think I need to lie down,' I mumbled, just before my legs buckled and gave way.

As everything went black, one thought spiralled through my mind: *Where is Gamble?*

You Big Bully

The next thing I knew I was lying on the ground, looking up at three blurry pink blobs. Slowly they came into focus and I recognised Mr Noblet, Miss Clegg and the old woman I'd seen by the tractor the day before. They were all looking concerned.

'Oh phew! He's awake,' said Mr Noblet. 'You're lucky Dan saw you from over the other side of the fence. Er . . . where is Dan?'

'Well, he was here a minute ago . . . ' began Miss Clegg. She looked over her shoulders, but he was nowhere to be seen.

I slowly sat up. My whole body stung and my face was sticky with what felt like blood. 'Is Darren OK?' I croaked.

'Darren's fine,' said Mr Noblet. 'What happened?'

'I'll tell you what happened!' came an angry voice from behind Mr Noblet. I sat up to see the farmer barrelling over towards us. He'd been chasing chickens around the field and now his red face looked just about ready to explode. 'This litt–'

'Now now, Jim,' interrupted the oldish woman, 'the doctor said you shouldn't get angry.'

'I told Daniel that this stupid survival camp was a bad idea all along,' the farmer snarled, pacing up and down. 'Useless, spoiled brat. I told him something like this would happen but he never listened. Mad Dan? *Thick* Dan, more like. I've a good mind . . . '

Suddenly Miss Clegg leapt to her feet. 'Don't you talk about my Dan like that,' she snapped.

'I'll talk about him how I like,' growled the farmer. 'He's my –'

He didn't get the chance to finish because Miss Clegg shoved her face right in front of his. 'I happen to think he's doing an amazing job. It's not his fault the two naughtiest kids on earth decided to break into your barn,' she snarled, 'so why don't you buzz off and go and milk your sheepdog?'

Milk his sheepdog?

I decided not to correct her on this point. And neither did the farmer because Miss Clegg gave him a fearsome belly-bounce, which caused him to stumble backwards. Shaking with rage, he growled, 'You've not heard the last of this!' before storming off into the field.

At that point the older woman cleared her throat. She seemed to have found the whole thing quite funny. 'Oh don't worry about my husband – he'll be alright when he calms down,' she said kindly.

‘So. You must be the young teaching assistant from the school. Daniel told me about you.’

‘Did he?’ squeaked Miss Clegg, like this was the most incredible news she’d ever heard.

‘I’m Daniel’s mother,’ said the older woman, shaking Miss Clegg’s hand. ‘We own the farm here, and all the land where Daniel runs his survival camp. Nice to meet you. Now I’d better go and help my husband round up the chickens.’

With that she turned on her heel and marched briskly off. Miss Clegg seemed very pleased with herself. ‘He told his mum about me!’ she announced to no one in particular.

Clinic

I’d never seen Miss Clegg so excited as she was on the way back to our campsite. She completely ignored the fact that I was in utter agony, and left Mr Noblet to help me across the field while she skipped ahead through the grass full of chickens, picking wild flowers.

Dan met us at the games pitch. When we got over the fence Mr Noblet asked him where he’d gone.

'Oh. Er. I was . . . you know. Didn't want to get in the way,' said Dan vaguely.

Vanya was standing by his shoulder. 'Hmmm,' she said. 'Actually, he ran away screaming as soon as he saw the chickens.'

Dan cracked his knuckles and muttered something under his breath.

'Are you OK, Roman?' Vanya asked.

I nodded pathetically.

Mr Noblet suggested that Dan should drive me to the nearest village to get checked out by a doctor.

'What? In my car?' he asked, horrified. 'Look at the state of him.'

I have to admit he did have a point. My clothes were filthy and torn, and I was completely covered in feathers and streaks of this white sloppy stuff I didn't really want to think about.

'Well. This is a survival centre,' said Vanya, raising her eyebrows. 'It's important you help him survive.'

Mad Dan huffed out his cheeks. 'Fine,' he agreed, reluctantly.

'I'll come too,' said Miss Clegg breathlessly.

We rode up the hill on Dan's quad bike, sending hundreds of chickens scattering everywhere. When we got to the car, he put bin bags on the leather seats and made me take off my wellies, which I suppose was fair enough. But I thought it was a bit much when he vacuumed me with the Dust Buster he kept in his boot before he let me get in.

On the way to the clinic, I sat all squashed up in the tiny back seat and said nothing. Even if I'd wanted to speak, I doubt anyone would've heard me. The engine was roaring loudly and in the front Miss Clegg was busy twiddling her hair and talking to Mad Dan. 'You didn't tell me your parents owned the farm,' she said.

'Huh,' said Mad Dan. He seemed deeply annoyed that I was in the car with them. 'Well. Dad thinks I should be a farmer. But I'm not. I'm a survivor. Luckily Mum realised it and helped me set up the survival centre. Keeping your own animals is cheating. I believe you should live off the land.'

'How marvellous,' said Miss Clegg, 'I can't wait to move out here and get that job working for you. It'll be amazing.'

Mad Dan seemed keen to change the subject, though and turned his attention to me, saying things like, 'Hey. Don't touch the leather,' and, 'Could you breathe a little bit less? You're fogging up the windows.'

In the village, I had to wait ages in the waiting room of the clinic. Miss Clegg bought us all sandwiches from the shop next door, which I guess was nice of her. Unfortunately, the only filling they had was chicken so I said I wasn't hungry. Dan said he preferred to eat fish he'd caught with his bare hands, but he still ate mine and his just the same.

In the clinic, the doctor wiped all my cuts with this horrible stingy liquid and told me I should take it easy for the rest of the day. Then they called my mum to check I'd had my injections. Mum was totally worried and said she wanted to come down there and hug me until my eyes popped out. Thankfully they told her I'd be fine and she'd be able to see me tomorrow anyway.

Afterwards, we drove back to camp. Dan put the top down on his car for this journey because he said I stank so bad I was making the leather on his seats crack.

'So what job will I be doing when I come and work for you?' asked Miss Clegg.

'Look,' replied Mad Dan, concentrating really hard on the road. 'Maybe we should . . . '

Miss Clegg sighed excitedly. 'I think I'd be really good at teaching survival skills to children.'

I had to stop myself from laughing at this point. I mean, Miss Clegg would be *rubbish* at that job. Firstly, she *hates* kids. One time she was helping in the dinner hall and I saw a plaster fall off her finger into the custard. I swear she stirred it in. Honestly! Then, even worse, she said to the other dinner lady: 'I bet you ten quid one of the little brats'll be stupid enough to eat it.'

And secondly, well, I don't want to be mean but come on! She's about as athletic as a dead slug.

Wisely, Dan said nothing.

Strange Sight

Dan parked up under the zip line tower and I limped down the hill to the tent. Here and there, a chicken would dart out of the bushes ahead of me, causing my heart to race.

When I got to the campsite, I was greeted by an extremely strange sight.

There were chickens everywhere, pecking at the

ground, perching on the tents and running in and out of the woods. Even though this was pretty creepy, it wasn't the strangest thing. Kevin 'Pukelear Missile' Harrison was sitting on one of those folding camp chairs outside Rosie Taylor's tent. And Rosie Taylor was sitting on his knee.

On his knee! She looked like a really horrific ventriloquist's dummy.

They both had stupid grins on their faces and there was a long queue of people standing in front of them, all waiting to get inside the tent.

I was just trying to figure out what on earth was going on when Vanya bounced over, looking really pleased to see me. 'Hey, Roman! I was worried about you. How are you doing?'

'I'm OK,' I said, even though I felt like I'd been scrubbed with a hedgehog. 'Have you seen Gamble? Is he alright?'

'Seems it,' said Vanya. 'He got back here anyway. Last I saw, he was trying to catch chickens with his bare hands.'

That was a relief. I still wasn't sure how he'd escaped earlier, but I could ask him later.

I nodded towards Kevin and Rosie and the queue of people. 'What's all that about?'

Rosie heard me and called over. 'OMG everyone. Roman's jealous!'

'Jealous of what?' I replied. My head was thumping and I was struggling to understand.

'Why of me and Kevin, of course,' she said, tickling his chin and standing up. 'It's official. We're an item.'

'An item?'

'Yes. As in, we're boyf and girlf.'

'It's true,' said Vanya. 'Ridiculous but true.'

Rosie gave a sickly smile. 'I've even announced it on Twitter. "Hashtag Kosie" is trending worldwide.'

'This makes no sense,' I said, my eyes aching, 'You called him the Grand Old Puke of York this morning.'

Rosie looked shocked and covered Kevin's ears. 'But that was then. Things change. He's so sweet. And he'll do *anything* for me. He even found me this chair. Isn't he adorable? And gorgeous. He reminds me of that Spanish pop star, Diego Marmite.'

Kevin grinned like a chimp.

The whole thing was bonkers: Kevin and Rosie? Together? I was just thinking that this was the stupidest thing I'd ever heard, when I was distracted by one of my classmates coming out of Rosie's tent.

'Next person,' announced Rosie, 'you've got five minutes. Start the timer, Kevin, you sweet little cherry tomato.'

Kevin pressed a button on his watch and the next person in the queue went inside the tent. 'What's going on?' I asked.

'I'm keeping people en-ter-tained,' Rosie said, as though she was talking to a complete moron. 'After you decided to make friends with the chickens, we've all had to sit around doing nothing 'til Dan gets back. Everyone was furious with you but I'm letting them play on my phone.'

'Really?' I said, raising an eyebrow. 'Why?'

'Because I'm the only person who brought one. Plus, I'm nice, of course.'

I almost choked on this. Rosie is the nastiest person I've ever met. One time she spread a rumour that she'd seen me 'snogging a dead tuna in the fish aisle at Tesco'.

'Word up, my people!' exclaimed Mad Dan, clapping his hands together from the end of the campsite. 'We've got catching up to do. Two minutes. Archery. You're gonna learn how to use a bow and arrow. One day it'll help you to catch your own dinner. Awoooooggaaaa!'

'I'm going for a lie down,' I said to Vanya, and wandered back to my tent. This was all too much to think about right now.

Is That All

As soon as I opened the zip, something flapped right up into my face. *A chicken!* Panicking, I staggered backwards, swinging my arms around at it before it dashed off into the campsite.

'Oi!' said Gamble from the corner of the tent, 'that was my dinner. Hang on. Are you alright? You're covered in cuts.'

I took a long look at his face. There wasn't even the tiniest mark on him. 'What happened?'

Gamble sniffed. 'Well, when it all kicked off, I legged it out of there and hid behind a cow.'

'A cow?'

Gamble's mouth spread into a wide smile and his head started twitching. 'Honestly it was ace. I fed her chicken nuggets out of my hands so she stayed still 'til all the chickens had gone. Then I saw the farmer so I sprant back here.'

'Sprinted,' I said. 'And what's this about a cow?'

He didn't seem to hear me. 'Hey. I know an

Amazing Fact about cows. You can lead one –'

'I'm not interested,' I said, surprised at how loud my voice was. 'You left me for dead while you hid behind a cow?'

'Well, no point in both of us getting hurt, was there?' he said. 'My uncle always says "every man for himself" when you're out on a robbery.'

'We weren't on a robbery,' I said. 'I was being mauled by chickens and you were making friends with a cow!'

He frowned. 'Hold on. Are you mad with me or summat?'

Exasperated, I huffed out my cheeks. 'Yes! Of course I am. *You* got us lost this morning. *You* used a chicken nugget to get us even more lost. *You* sent all those chickens into a flapping frenzy. Then *you* disappeared.'

'Oh,' he said, picking his nose then sucking his finger clean like it was a flipping Cornetto. 'Sorry about that. I didn't mean to.'

I shook my head and lay down on my sleeping bag. Gamble stood there for a few minutes not saying anything before he finally got the hint and left.

Vanya was right – why *was* I friends with him?

All he does is ruin everything. He once told me he'd accidentally broken his pet tortoise. I'm not kidding. What kind of a person could *break* a tortoise?

I kicked at the bag of frozen nuggets that he'd stolen the night before, scattering a few of them across the groundsheet. Then I closed my eyes and tried to get some rest.

For the next hour I slipped in and out of sleep until I was woken by the zip being pulled up. 'Hey, you missed archery, it was well wicked, I almost shot a chicken,' exclaimed Gamble excitedly. He doesn't really seem to understand that people might stay mad with him for more than two seconds.

When I didn't say anything he squinted at me. 'Don't be like that,' he begged.

'Leave me alone,' I snapped back.

Gamble looked sad, like a baby who'd just been mugged for its rattle. 'Oh come on. Don't you want to come to quad biking? They sent me to see if you fancied it.'

Of course I wanted to come to quad biking. Quad biking sounded amazing. But obviously I didn't want to go with *him*. 'No,' I grunted, rolling over and biting my lip, 'I'll stay here.'

There was a long pause. Then, his voice wavering, Gamble croaked, 'Does this mean you don't want to be mates any more?'

I didn't reply. He slipped out, the zip closed and I was on my own again.

Evening (and Night)

When I Survived the New Tribal Chief

The chicken nugget ambush was now moving into a new stage. Along with Gamble, they'd caused the flap-o-rama in the barn, and my skin was shredded as a reminder. It seemed like I was no longer friends with Gamble, which might've been a good thing. But I'd learn soon enough that a desperate Gamble is a dangerous Gamble. Meanwhile, though, and unknown to me, the nasty nuggets were plotting new attacks from different, surprising directions.

I didn't leave the tent until after tea-time. Vanya smuggled me back some chips from the canteen.

Delighted to finally have something different to eat (even if they were floppy and cold like a dead person's fingers) I wolfed them down in about three seconds. She really was a good friend. After I'd finished, we headed over to the campfire together.

'Your mate's been acting a bit weird this afternoon,' she said.

'Gamble?' I asked. 'More weird than normal, you mean?'

Vanya shrugged. 'Quiet and depressed. There was a food fight in the canteen and he didn't even join in.'

That didn't sound like Gamble at all. Normally in that situation he'd have probably made a deadly weapon out of a sharpened spoon and some apple crumble. Maybe I *had* been a bit harsh on him. For a moment I felt bad. Then I looked at my chicken-pecked arms and thought about how he'd hidden behind a cow and left me for dead, and I very quickly got over it.

When we got to the campfire, most of the class were already sitting on the logs. Over on the far side of the fire pit, Gamble had saved a space for me. He pointed at it, his face hopeful. When I pretended I hadn't seen him, his shoulders slumped.

Despite the fact I was still cross with him, I felt bad about this – when Darren's sad he has a face like a wounded kitten.

On another log, Rosie Taylor was perched on Kevin 'Pukelear Missile' Harrison's knee again. Unfortunately there was nowhere else to sit so Vanya and I had to park ourselves nearby.

'Do you mind getting off for a moment?' Kevin said to Rosie in a strained voice. 'My belly's a bit full from dinner.'

Rosie turned round, a big fake smile plastered across her face, and placed her hand on Kevin's cheek. 'But, darling. You're my boyfriend. You've got to do what I tell you, remember?'

'I really don't feel great . . . ' Kevin whined.

'Listen,' hissed Rosie, suddenly squeezing his cheek tightly. Her voice was no longer all lovey-dovey. 'This trouser suit was hand-stitched in Italy. I'm not sitting on some mingtastic log.'

Kevin was turning slightly green. 'But there's a chance I might . . . '

'Don't you even think about it,' she snapped. 'You might be my Forever Babe, but if you puke on me ever again I swear I'll train one of those chickens to savage you in your sleep.'

Kevin gulped.

Rosie pressed her face right into his. 'Now if you feel the need to throw up, you'll just have to choke on it. Is that alright, gorgeous?'

For the last bit, her voice went all gooey and soppy again, and she fluffed up his hair like he was a little dog in a handbag. Kevin gulped and nodded his head nervously.

'I don't think that relationship's going to last long, do you?' whispered Vanya.

I snorted but managed to turn it into a cough when Rosie stared daggers at me.

The campfire was pretty much the same as on Monday. We sang stupid songs (e.g. *Wiggle Waggle Wig, Your Bottom is Big*, and *Flip Flap Flop, Who's Done a Plop?* etc.) then had the vote for Tribal Chief.

To my amazement, only one person was nominated – Rosie Taylor. Apparently everyone was over the moon that she'd let them play with her phone and she was now the most popular person in the universe!

When she won the vote, Mad Dan tried to put the feathery headdress on her but she slapped his hand away. 'You'll ruin my hair,' she snapped. Then she stood up to give a massive speech, which was a bit unnecessary.

'I'd like to say thank you to my pet pug Cheryl for always loving me,' she said, wiping away the tears. 'To my personal stylist for always making me look so fabulous; to my eternal boyf Kevin for always doing what I say . . . ' She simpered at Kevin when she said this and everyone went mental. 'And also to my favourite reality TV star, Tabitha Bowel, for inspiring me on this journey. Hopefully this will be my first step to becoming the celebrity that the world deserves. Thank you for worshipping me. I'm so lucky to have fans like you. Mwah. Mwah.'

Unbelievably, everyone clapped.

'Now, of course,' she continued, raising her hand, 'as your leader, I must create an ickle-wickle new rule for you to follow. My rule is that Roman will slop out the leftovers after breakfast tomorrow.'

'What?' I exclaimed. That was ridiculous, not to mention totally cruel and unfair.

'Gotta do it, bro,' said Mad Dan, looking pleased that I was annoyed. 'We can't survive as a tribe unless we got rules.'

Rosie gave me a smarmy smile and plonked herself down on Kevin's lap again.

I ran my fingers through my hair. How typical of Rosie. And how typical of Mad Dan to let her do it!

'Could've been worse,' said Vanya, behind her hand.

I smiled weakly back. The next morning I'd find out that she was quite wrong.

Depressed

After Rosie had announced her new rule, Mad Dan stood up on his log. 'Bosh, dudes,' he called, and everyone yelled *bosh!* in reply. 'So I gotta go change the sticks on my little shelter. You guys get a good night's sleep 'cos tomorrow's your last day. You're going home at lunchtime.'

Everyone went *awwwwww.*

Personally, I'd had about enough and was ready to go home there and then.

Miss Clegg crept over to Dan. 'Maybe you should build me a shelter outside tonight,' she said. 'You know. Near yours. Then I can get used to sleeping in the forest before I start my new job.'

Mad Dan cleared his throat and shuffled his feet around on the ground. 'Not sure that's totally necessary . . . '

At that moment, Gamble started tugging on Miss Clegg's sleeve. 'Miss, miss. You know you're my teaching assistant? Well, I think I need to talk to you about something.'

Miss Clegg shook him off and looked at him like he'd just slithered out of a toilet. 'Look, Darren. I'm only going to be your TA for another twelve hours.'

'Er . . . *what*?' said Mr Noblet, who'd overheard her.

Miss Clegg flicked her hair off her face. 'I'm not coming back on the bus tomorrow. I feel alive here with Dan and I'm not working with this little turd for another minute longer than I have to.'

'But . . . ' spluttered Mr Noblet.

'You can't!' said Darren.

'Tough,' said Miss Clegg. 'Time you got used to figuring things out on your own. And anyway. I'm busy talking to . . . '

But when she turned around, Mad Dan had snuck off. As she hurried off to look for him, with Mr Noblet following her, Gamble slumped back down to the floor and stared into the glowing coals of the fire. He looked like the last shrivelled-up satsuma in the fruit bowl.

I wasn't going to feel sorry for him, though. No way.

On the walk back to the campsite, Vanya and I could see hundreds of chickens flapping up to roost in the low branches. 'How's the farmer going to catch them all?' I asked.

'He wasn't having much luck earlier,' she replied. 'He got a few to follow him by putting out food but he gave up in the end. There are just too many.'

Near the tents, we said goodbye to each other. Afterwards I brushed my teeth with my finger in the shower block. There was no sign of Gamble in our tent but Kevin 'Pukelear Missile' Harrison was already tucked up in his sleeping bag. He wouldn't shut up, going on and on about how *amazing* Rosie Taylor was. ' . . . and she said when she's famous I can carry her bags for her and she's so beautiful it makes me want to puke and we're going to meet up tomorrow before breakfast and. . . '

In the end I folded my pillow over my head so I didn't have to listen any more. *What had got into Kevin?* Had he puked out his brain *and* his eyeballs or something? Rosie has a face like a dropped pie.

Not that looks are everything, of course. But

Rosie is also literally the meanest person who's ever lived. One time in ICT she made a Powerpoint presentation called: '10 Reasons Why Roman Garstang Is a Friendless Weirdo'. The reasons included: '1 - He is a massive freak' (not fair); '4 – He smells like a giraffe's undies' (not true); and '10 – His favourite hobby is hanging around shops, sniffing the milk' (not fair *and* not true).

I'd been lying there for about half an hour, with Kevin's droning voice only partly muffled by the pillow, when Gamble came back into the tent. He lightly tapped me on the shoulder.

'Roman,' he whispered and I slowly sat up. He looked like he'd been crying.

'What is it?' I asked wearily.

'I wanted to say sorry so I brought you a treat.'

I sagged back down onto my uncomfortable mat. 'Is it a nipple ring?'

'No.'

'A tattoo?'

'No.'

'A chicken nugget?'

'No.'

'A whole chicken, perhaps?'

'It's here,' he said, tapping the bulging front pocket

of his shirt. 'I just wanted to make it up to you.'

I rolled back over. 'No, thanks. I'm sorry, Darren, but you just cause me too many problems. I think I can have better friends.'

'What? Like that Vanya?' he said, his voice rising with tears and anger.

I turned to face him again. 'Yes, actually. She's nice to me and she's not completely nuts and useless and . . . hey . . . where are you going?'

He was already halfway out of the tent. When he turned round, his face was streaked with dirty tears. 'Don't worry about me any more. You're not the only one who can find a new friend!'

With that he was gone, the bag of chicken nuggets tucked under his arm.

I lay there for a moment, starting to feel bad. The problem with Gamble is he can't really help himself from being the way he is. He's a bit like a massive, naughty puppy that's not been house-trained yet. Maybe I had been too harsh on him. Maybe I should give him another chance.

'Go after him,' said Kevin.

'Eh?' I said.

Kevin sat up. 'I mean, a nice person like Rosie would go after him. She's so kind and lovely. Earlier today she even helped that farmer put out food to get the chickens back and . . . '

Hmmm, I thought, blocking out the rest of his story. I suppose he was a bit right. The least I could do was make sure Gamble was OK. Plus, if I had to listen to one more word about how amazing Rosie Taylor was, I might actually throw up myself. As quick as I could, I put on my wellies and chased after Gamble across the campsite.

I called after him, but he was way ahead of me, slinking between the trees, along the paths and off towards the games field. There was a full moon though, so I could just about see the back of his grubby white shirt as it disappeared round bends and under branches.

When I finally caught up with Gamble, he'd climbed over the fence and was standing alone in one of the farmer's fields, like a weird little scare-crow. Beyond him, the lights were blazing out of the farmhouse. It was only when I got up close that I realised he was stroking a cow's nose. Its black body was almost invisible in the darkness. Scared, I took a couple of steps back.

'Go away!' Gamble said.

'But . . . ' I protested, struggling for breath.

Then I noticed something. 'Darren, are you feeding that cow . . . *raw chicken nuggets*?'

'Course I am,' said Gamble, like this was the most normal thing in the world. 'She loves 'em.'

He held out another one in his palm and the cow greedily licked it up.

'Are cows *meant* to eat those?' I said. 'I thought they ate grass.'

'She's my new best mate. Best mates don't complain when other best mates bring 'em stuff. Now leave us alone or I'll get her to squirt milk on you.'

I sighed. There's no point trying to get through to Gamble when he's in this mood. Honestly, one time in class Miss Clegg told him off for colouring in Kevin's teeth with a highlighter pen and Gamble hid inside an upturned wheelbarrow in the school garden for the rest of the day.

As I trudged back across the field, my eyes were drawn towards the farmhouse. I couldn't believe what I saw. Through one of the windows, I could see Mad Dan. He was wearing a fluffy white bathrobe. There was this thick white paste on his face, like my mum wears every night to keep her skin looking young and beautiful. He bent down in front of the window and stood up, fluffing a pillow. Then he took off his robe to reveal his pyjamas before pulling the curtains shut. The light went out.

Wow! I thought. Mad Dan, so-called survival expert, was sleeping in a bed. In a house. Vanya was right all along. He didn't live in the woods at all. What a fraud!

When I got back to the tent, I crawled straight into my sleeping bag. I was a bit worried about Gamble but what could I do about it? He'd probably come back to the tent when he was bored. Exhausted from everything that had happened that day, I fell asleep almost straight away.

WEDNESDAY

Morning

When I Survived a Wet Alarm Clock

That night I had a really weird dream. I was an ice cream and there was this giant baby licking me with its huge floppy tongue and I tried to scream but its tongue tore off my nose and mouth then . . .

I woke up.

Something really *was* licking me.

Something big.

Something with a huge long tongue and very bad breath.

I rolled over and blinked three times against the half-light through the tent and – *oh my word* . . .

I was face to face with a cow.

A *cow,* for crying out loud!

It leant down and licked my face again.

Rigid with terror, I screamed.

'Oh, you're awake,' said Gamble cheerily, from somewhere behind the cow. 'Say hello to Gusher.'

'Mooooo!' said Gusher. It stepped forwards, its back pressing against the side of the tent.

'Yowwww!' I cried, as a hoof landed on my knee.

I should never have opened my mouth, though, because, at that exact moment, the cow stepped forward again and one of its udders landed in my mouth. Its *udder*! Oh it was horrible, like a big milky, rubbery finger flapping around my lips.

I scrambled out from under Gusher and rolled across the tent, furiously wiping my face. 'What on earth is going on?' I screamed. The cow was right in the middle of the tent. This was the only place it could stand without touching the roof and sides.

Gamble grinned. He'd cheered up completely from last night and was back to his crazy, excitable self. 'Well, I was out there most of the night and when I turned round to come home this morning, Gusher just followed me, so I gave her another chicken nugget and she followed me some more and before I knew it we were both back here and the bag was almost empty.'

I shook my head. 'You gave her the whole bag? Are you sure that was a good idea?'

'Course,' said Gamble, patting the bulging top pocket of his shirt. 'I got you a treat and you turned your nose up at it. Best mates don't do that.'

'But . . . '

He held the last couple of nuggets out in his hand. Gusher slurped them up hungrily and swallowed them. 'See. That's what mates *should* do.'

'I'm *not* going to eat from your hand,' I said. It could've been literally anywhere.

'Huh. Well, I'm gonna see if Mr Noblet will let me bring her back to school on the coach.'

'You're insane,' I said.

'Yeah, great, innit!' beamed Gamble.

I was about to tell him that this wasn't actually a compliment when he did a seriously disturbing thing. He bent down and calmly milked the cow into his plastic cup.

Milked it.

As in . . . you know . . . squeezed milk out of its *boobs*. I watched in absolute horror as he lifted the cup to his mouth and drained it in one go.

'Ahhhhh! Delicious!' he said, wiping away his milk moustache and holding up the cup to me. 'She's a miles better mate than you ever were. You *never* let me milk you.'

I had no idea what to say to this. For a few seconds my mouth opened and closed like a broken electric garage. 'Look,' I said finally, trying to move the conversation away from the whole milking thing. 'If we get caught with a cow in here we'll get in tonnes of trouble. That farmer will go b–'

I didn't get the chance to finish because, at that exact moment, the cow lifted up its tail and, with alarming power, weed all over my sleeping bag.

'Uuurghhh! This can't be happening!' I cried.

'She's always doing that,' smiled Gamble. 'That's why I call her Gusher.'

'Then why did you bring her into our tent?' I said. 'We sleep here, for heaven's sake. Kevin, back me up on this. Kevin . . . ?'

But he wasn't there. I hadn't noticed before but his sleeping bag was empty. He mustn't have been here when Gamble brought the cow in – which was probably a good thing. He'd only have thrown up all over it.

As I tried to figure out where Kevin might have

gone, there was a knock on the side of the tent. 'What's going on in there?' said Miss Clegg. 'Are you fighting?'

She must've seen the tent walls bulging out when Gusher was moving around. Luckily the cow was now lying down so Miss Clegg wouldn't be able to see anything. For the time being at least . . .

I looked at Gamble, my eyes open wide. 'What are we going to do?'

'Simple,' whispered Gamble. 'I'm gonna jump on Gusher's back and ride her out of here, crush Miss Clegg beneath her hooves then go on the run.'

'Ridiculous,' I said.

'No, it's not,' tutted Gamble, 'I've already figured it out. I can teach Gusher to juggle.'

I shook my head.

'I'll make a fortune,' he continued. 'How many juggling cows do you know of?'

'They don't juggle because they DON'T HAVE HANDS!' I replied.

'She could have mine. I don't need 'em.'

'Moooooo,' said Gusher, as she began nosing around the empty bag of chicken nuggets on the floor.

'What was that?' said Miss Clegg from outside.

I unzipped the tent just far enough to poke my head out. 'That was . . . er . . . me,' I stuttered, struggling to think of what to say next. 'I said . . . "*Oooooooh,* it's . . . lovely in this tent". But we're not quite ready to come out yet.'

'Well, I've only got three hours left as Darren's teaching assistant so as far as I'm concerned he can do whatever he wants, as long as he doesn't kill anyone.'

With that, she turned and waddled off. This was a lucky escape. But if Mr Noblet or anyone else came along, we might not get away with it again.

'I'm getting out of here,' I said to Gamble, ducking my head back inside. 'Just make sure the cow isn't here when I get back.'

'Fat chance,' said Gamble.

I slipped out of the tent and into the morning sunlight. Around the campsite, a few of my classmates were climbing out of their tents as well, stretching and chatting to each other.

Vanya bounded over. She looked at me, concerned. 'Are you alright?'

I was just trying to figure out what to say when Gamble followed me outside, dragging my sleeping bag behind him then zipping up the tent. 'Oi, *ex*-best mate,' he said, dumping the sleeping bag on the floor. 'You're not leaving this in the tent all day. It's covered in wee. Get rid of it.'

I looked from Vanya to the sleeping bag, then back to Vanya. She looked back at me with an open mouth.

'It's OK,' Mr Noblet said, strolling over and putting his hand on my shoulder, 'everyone's done it before.'

'Er . . . no we haven't,' said Rosie, striding over with her hair in curlers. 'Roman's lost control. Class-tastic!'

As Rosie snapped away with her phone, everybody came over and started pointing and laughing at me. My sleeping bag looked like it had been dropped in a swimming pool. I wasn't a bed-wetter; I was a bed-*flooder*.

'I can explain . . . ' I said, even though I couldn't. What could I do? If I told the truth, everyone would know about the cow in the tent. Even though I wasn't exactly best pals with Gamble any more, part of me still didn't want to land him in trouble for cow-napping.

'I'll leave you to it,' said Vanya, looking at me uneasily as she edged away.

Rosie shoved her face right into mine. 'Oh. And before you try and wiggle out of it, you've got to slop out after breakfast, remember. So long, sucker!'

She wandered away, cackling as she uploaded the photo of my soggy sleeping bag onto the internet. Could this 'holiday' get any worse?

Of course it could.

Slopping Out

Because it was our last morning, Mad Dan cooked us bacon and eggs. Of course, I wasn't allowed any even though I was absolutely starving. Dan seemed delighted to fling a few cold chicken nuggets from the day before onto my plate.

This was the final straw. 'Oh, come on,' I said. 'Why does everyone have to be so cruel to me?'

'Oooh. Someone's tired,' cooed Rosie from further along the queue. 'Hard to sleep in a puddle, eh?'

Mad Dan raised an eyebrow at me. 'You know what, kid? If you ever wanna learn how to survive, you gotta deal with your attitude problem.'

Seething to myself, I snatched my tray and went to find a seat. Because Vanya thought I was a bed-wetter, I was too embarrassed to sit next to her so I decided to sit on my own in the corner. Neither Gamble nor Kevin had turned up yet.

'Survivors,' announced Mad Dan after everyone had sat down. 'You've almost made it. This morning, we'll do some brutal climbing and abseiling then we'll pack up your tents and you'll head back home as heroes. Awooga!'

Awooga! said everyone.

Miss Clegg lumbered over to him. 'Morning,' she said.

'Yo, babe,' replied Mad Dan.

'I wanted to chat about my new job, so I came to see you in your shelter this morning but you weren't there,' she said.

Mad Dan spluttered. 'Oh. Yeah. I was . . . er . . . out . . . hunting.'

'Hunting?'

'Yep,' he said. 'For . . . moose.'

'Moose? Do we have them in our country?'

'No . . . we don't. Probably why I didn't catch any,' said Mad Dan, smiling.

I knew of course that this wasn't true. He'd slept in his parents' farmhouse. Why did he have to keep trying to impress her by lying?

Mad Dan seemed desperate to change the subject.

'Anyhow, so I went to see my mum. Looks like we've got a job lined up for you,' he said.

'Oh *wow*!' said Miss Clegg, her hands clasped over her mouth.

'Now, I gotta warn you . . . ' said Mad Dan, but Miss Clegg wasn't listening.

'Living in the wild . . . teaching people how to survive . . . finally escaping that frightful boy!'

Looking frustrated, Dan huffed out his cheeks and turned his attention to the class. 'Awooga, survivors,' he called, clapping his hands together. 'Who's on slop-out duty today?'

'The human water fountain,' said Rosie, pointing towards me. A few people sniggered. Vanya looked over at me sympathetically.

Reluctantly, I swallowed one final morsel of nugget and plodded over to the slop-out bucket. While the last people tipped their leftovers into it, Kevin 'Grand Old Puke of York' Harrison finally staggered into the canteen. He was out of breath and pale, and he had big black rings around his eyes. *Where had he been?* With a typically dramatic flourish, Rosie leapt to her feet and flung her arms round him. As she did so, though, she glanced mockingly at me over his shoulder.

I shook my head and walked away.

My job was to carry the plastic slop-out bucket back through the woods, across the campsite and up to the big wheelie bin in the car park. It wasn't particularly heavy but the delicious smell of leftover bacon coming from it was torturous.

I noticed on my way past that our tent had been flattened. *Huh*, I thought. The cow must've crushed it. *How typical*. Predictably enough, Gamble and Gusher were nowhere to be seen. I tutted and carried on.

When I was halfway up the hill, I realised something. The whole time I'd been walking I hadn't seen a single chicken. Yesterday there were thousands of them everywhere but now they'd all disappeared. I guessed that they'd either spread out for miles, or that the farmer had somehow managed to round them all up.

Unfortunately, both of these ideas were completely and utterly wrong . . .

NOOOOOOOOO!

As I approached the car park, I finally saw the first chicken. It was making its way up the hill. For a moment it paused to peck at the floor then carried on going. Then I saw another. And another. And another. In fact, there were loads of them and they all seemed to be moving in the same direction – up the hill and past the wheelie bins. They were all pecking the ground as they went.

Although this was a little odd, I didn't think too much of it at first. I dragged the bucket over to the wheelie bin, which was right at the top of the path, then hoisted the waste inside.

And that's when I heard it.

Clucking.

A *lot* of clucking.

At first I thought it was coming from the zip wire tower but when I looked around the side of the bin I realised it was coming from Mad Dan's car. I sprinted over, following what I realised was a trail of leftover food that led right up to the sportscar.

When I reached the car I felt my face go pale. To my horror, mountains of leftover food had been poured across the seats. But that wasn't the worst of it.

There were chickens everywhere.

I swear there must've been about forty of them

in the car, pecking at the food and anything else they could find. The leather upholstery was scratched and covered in little white splats. Foam was spewing out of a rip in one of the seats and two chickens were pulling it out with their beaks. The car's convertible roof was still down, and another chicken was trapped inside the folded material. It was struggling to escape, tearing away with its sharp talons. An egg had broken in the footwell and sticky yolk rubbed into the floor. Meanwhile, more chickens strutted into the car park, pecking at bits of food on the ground and heading towards the car.

A terrible realisation came over me. Someone had done this on purpose. They had laid a trail of leftover food to attract the chickens then dumped the rest into the car. And here *I* was, standing on my own with an empty bucket that had just come from the kitchen.

This wouldn't look good. In fact, it was going to look really, really bad.

But, if there's one thing I've learned, it's that things can always get worse.

'Oh no!' screamed a voice behind me. 'We're too late!'

I froze. Rosie was running up the hill. Striding

behind her came Mad Dan, Miss Clegg, Mr Noblet and the rest of our class.

'What have you done?' yelled Mad Dan, as he reached the car. It took me a moment to realise he was talking to me.

'I'm so sorry,' said Rosie to Dan. 'If only we could've raised the alarm sooner. I should never have got him to slop out. He said he was going to do something terrible to the car, didn't he, Kevin my little darling?'

Kevin gulped. 'Well . . . '

Rosie kissed him on the cheek. Kevin went red and looked at the floor, avoiding my gaze. 'Yes,' he mouthed.

I'd been set up.

I spluttered to try and say something but Rosie interrupted. 'He's had it in for you right from the start, Dan,' she continued. 'Ever since you made him share a tent with that awful skunk, Darren Gamble. He blamed you for forcing him to eat chicken nuggets, and for making him clean your car. And you heard the way he spoke to you at breakfast. He's a very bitter, twisted person. I've heard him talking to that weirdo Vanya about you too. They reckon you're not even a real survival expert, even though we all know you are. He must've laid a trail for all the chickens then dumped the rest of the food in the car. Hashtag – *busted.*'

'That's not true,' I croaked but Mad Dan didn't hear me because he was too busy kneeling on the ground, weeping. He let out a scream at the top of his voice: 'NOOOOOOOOO!' At this, a couple of chickens fluttered out of the car and began to peck the ground around his feet.

Mad Dan turned to face me. His eyes were wild and his face twisted with rage. 'You've destroyed my beautiful car!' he yelled, his vast muscles bristling with anger. I edged backwards, absolutely terrified, but I was too slow and he grabbed me by the collar.

'But, darling,' said Miss Clegg to him, 'I thought you said you'd rather ride a wild horse?'

'Of course I wouldn't!' he cried. 'I love this car more than anything in the world. I only say those things so people believe I'm a survival expert who lives outdoors.'

'You mean . . . ' began Miss Clegg.

'I knew it!' said Vanya, clapping her hands together.

'I live in the farmhouse,' he said, looking at Miss Clegg.

Admitting this out loud seemed to have a sudden effect on Dan. The anger suddenly drained from his face. He let go of my collar and stared at the ground. To my amazement, tears began welling up in his eyes. 'I'm scared of animals. That's why I couldn't be a farmer. But I always *wanted* to be tough, and to live on the land. That's why I went to the gym, and pretended I'd been in the Special Forces, and started the survival camp. I'm a wimp, really. I mean, I like the activities. I just don't like the creepy crawlies . . . '

Miss Clegg looked confused. 'But Dan. You said th–'

She was interrupted by the farmer. 'Magnificent!' he cried, striding across the car park with his wife behind him. 'You've rounded up my chickens. Well done, son! And I've always thought you weren't cut out for the farming life. I'm proud of you, lad. Finally I'm proud of you.'

Mad Dan looked at him like a stray dog that had finally found a home. 'What? Really?'

A great big smile was stretched across the farmer's red cheeks. 'Course. Good work. We'll have 'em back in the barn in no time.'

He slapped Mad Dan on the shoulder.

'And here's the girl who's coming to work for us on the farm,' said his wife, appearing by Miss Clegg's side.

Miss Clegg looked surprised. 'I'm *what*?'

'Hasn't he told you the good news yet?' grinned the farmer. 'You're going to be the chief chicken-plucker. Dan said you're keen to move out here and I'm delighted to have you on board.'

Miss Clegg swung her eyes towards Mad Dan. 'You told me I'd be working for you. At the survival centre. You said I could be free.'

Mad Dan scratched at the floor with his foot. 'I didn't really . . . It was you who thought . . . '

'I'm not plucking flipping chickens!' she yelled.

'It won't just be plucking them . . . ' said Mad Dan, looking terrified.

'You'll be pulling their guts out too!' said the farmer, as though this was a really fabulous job.

'Please don't be cross,' said Dan, quietly. 'I was going to tell you before you started. Honest.'

Miss Clegg looked like she was going to crush Dan's skull.

'Excuse me!' announced Rosie Taylor, pulling at Mr Noblet's sleeve. 'I know you're all having a moment or whatever but let's not forget. Roman has just ruined this car so, you know, can you just tell him off or expel him or hit him with a stick or something?'

For a moment I thought about facing up to my problems. But only for a moment. Then I realised that this would be a completely stupid thing to do. So, instead, I decided to leg it.

The only place to go was the zip line tower but when I reached the platform at the top I stopped in my tracks. I wasn't the only one up there.

The Problem With Having Half the Facts

Gamble was sitting on the floor with his plastic bag. His fact book was open next to him. But, most surprisingly of all, Gusher was up there too. She was cramped into the small space, shuffling her hooves impatiently.

'What are you doing up here?' I asked. 'And more to the point, what's *she* doing up here?'

'I'm hiding from you,' he said, not looking at me.

Gusher let out a sorrowful moo. Her head was kind of lolling about and she seemed agitated. 'Are you sure she's OK?' I asked. 'She doesn't look well.'

Gamble sniffed. 'I think it might be all the chicken nuggets. Her belly's a bit swollen. But why are *you* here?'

'If you must know,' he huffed, finally looking at me. 'I was gonna hot-wire Mad Dan's car and drive off with Gusher in the back, but then I saw Kevin coming up the hill. I didn't want anyone to see me, right, but I remembered that fact from my book – 'you can lead a cow upstairs' – so I got Gusher to come up here with me til he'd gone. Then the mad thing was that Kevin poured all this food in the car and I dunno why he did it.'

Kevin.

I let this sink in for a moment.

Of course! So *that* was why Rosie wanted me to slop out. And *that's* where Kevin had been this morning during breakfast. He'd said last night he was planning to meet her. It was so obvious. Rosie had got *him* to lay the trail for the chickens so they'd ruin the car then she'd made sure that *I'd* be caught red-handed. No wonder Kevin couldn't look at me.

'Darren,' I said, my voice shaky. 'Please can you

tell this story to everyone downstairs? They think I destroyed Dan's car.'

Darren frowned at me. 'So you've got in trouble for something you didn't do?'

'Exactly.'

'And you want me to get you out of trouble by telling them the truth?'

'Yes.'

Darren squinted, like he was thinking really hard. 'Er . . . no.'

'No?'

'Well, firstly I'm stuck,' he said. 'You see, I never read the end of that fact.'

He pointed to a fact on the open page of his fact book. Immediately I remembered it from the coach. Well, actually, that's not true. I remembered the *first half* of it – the part Gamble had read out before he'd pulled a moony at that lorry. The full fact is:

'You can lead a cow upstairs but ***you can't lead it downstairs***.'

'I ain't going anywhere without Gusher. And I ain't gonna speak to any of them. I'm gonna live up here forever and eat pigeons and . . . '

I could hear footsteps coming up the stairs.

Someone knew I was here. 'Please, Darren,' I said urgently. 'I'm sorry.'

It was too late.

The farmer had reached the platform. 'What on earth is going on?' he cried, rushing to Gusher and checking her over. 'What have you been doing to my prize cow?'

Sheepishly, Gamble held up the now-empty bag of chicken nuggets. The farmer snatched it from his hands and his eyes nearly popped out of his head. 'Her belly's bloated,' he said, patting her sides. 'When was the last time she had a poo?'

Gamble shut one eye. 'I don't think she's ever had one.'

The farmer's eyebrows shot up and he got straight on the phone.

Within half an hour, there were two fire engines in the car park, along with a vet, a police car and a TV crew from the local news. Police tape was stretched around the scene and our whole class was gathered behind it, looking upwards at the platform.

Above us, a couple of firemen and the vet were fitting a harness under Gusher's belly. Meanwhile, one of the fire engines was extending a crane arm to the landing in order to pick her up using the harness. From what I could gather, the plan was to hoist her off the landing and lay her down carefully on the grass by the car park.

I was standing with Gamble, who was desperately biting his fingernails and looking up at the platform. They'd literally had to drag him down the stairs to separate him from Gusher.

On the ground near us, the TV crew were setting up in front of the building. A man with perfect hair and white teeth was speaking to the camera. 'Drama here at the Farm View Survival Centre, where an incredible rescue is about to take place. Let's find out what some onlookers think.'

He pushed the microphone in front of Rosie, who'd been hanging around him the whole time. 'What can you tell us about the situation here?'

Rosie smiled her usual sickly smile. 'Hi, World. I'm Rosie and the situation is that I'm really hoping to work in television when I'm older so how are you all doing?'

The man coughed. 'Right. Well. Er. I meant the situation with the cow.'

'Oh right. Yeah. Whatever. Look. Why don't they just push it off? They're gonna turn it into beef-burgers sooner or later.'

The presenter's mouth dropped open.

'Can I sing a song?' asked Rosie.

'What?' said the presenter.

'I think some record company bosses might be watching. This could be my big break.'

The presenter waved his hand back and forth in front of his throat. 'Cut.'

'We'll chat later,' simpered Rosie, as the camera panned round to the tower.

Up on the landing, the crew had wrapped the harness round the cow and the crane hook was slowly being lowered so they could attach it.

Gamble dug his nails into my shoulder. Even though it wrecked, I didn't ask him to let go because I could see how upset he was. 'They're going to hurt her,' he said. I noticed his face was streaked with tears and his voice was all crackly.

I was about to tell Darren that they knew what they were doing when he suddenly shot under the police tape and darted back up towards the tower. To my surprise, I felt really worried for him. I quickly turned to Miss Clegg.

'Miss Clegg, I think Darren's gone to do something stupid,' I said.

Miss Clegg waved her hand at me dismissively.

'Chickens . . . ' she cried, lost in her own little world. 'How could he think I'd want to pluck chickens?'

After that I rushed to tell Mr Noblet about Gamble but the farmer stormed over to him before I got the chance. 'I've just spoken to the vet!' he roared. 'That cow is seriously sick. Her belly's all swollen and she can't go to the toilet. D'you know what those little maggots have been feeding her?'

I gulped.

The crane hook had been attached to the harness and now it was being slowly lifted upwards. The rope went taut, then the cow's feet were gently lifted off the ground. The crowd cheered. Inch by inch, the cow was taken up and over the rail of the zip line tower, before hanging in the air, fifty feet above the ground. Everyone gasped as Gusher rotated slowly.

One of the firemen on the landing was shouting down. 'Move the crowd back, we'll lower her down over there, on the field.'

The ground crew edged us all backwards, leaving a clear path from the crane to the edge of the grass. They were about to lower the cow when a police officer on the ground pointed up and shouted. 'Stop! Who's this idiot?'

We all looked up. *This idiot* was Gamble, of course, who was standing on top of the safety rail around the platform.

'I won't leave you on your own, Gusher!' he cried, and then he dived off the fence, landing on top of Gusher's back and clinging to her neck as she span wildly around.

'This is incredible!' cried the TV presenter, before putting his hand over the microphone and whispering to the camera crew. 'Make sure you've got the ground covered in case he falls.'

'Darren!' I wailed. My stomach flipped over. I was terrified for him.

'Quickly! Bring it down! Before he falls!' shouted one of the firemen to the crane operator. The crane arm moved down towards the field.

Suddenly, Gusher slipped in the harness. The rope swung forward and back then began spinning out of control. Gusher was just about held in place by her front legs and Gamble was desperately hanging onto her back. They were twenty feet above the ground. The more the cow panicked, the more the rope swung.

Until finally she slipped.

Both boy and cow tumbled through the air for what felt like an eternity. My breath caught in my throat. Everything went into slow motion. Gamble slammed into the grass and landed with a *thud*. Gusher fell in front of him.

But, instead of landing, she bounced.

Seriously. She'd landed on one of the trampolines by the adventure playground. She flew back up into the air and then began to plummet to earth before connecting with a crunch on Mad Dan's car. Luckily, the air bag exploded and gave her a cushioned landing.

'Darren!' cried Miss Clegg, sprinting through the crowd.

'Gamble!' I yelled.

'My cow!' screamed the farmer.

'My car!' howled Mad Dan.

I reached Darren at exactly the same moment as Miss Clegg. She knelt down beside him and rested his head on her lap. 'Speak to me, Darren! Speak to me!'

Darren did better than that. He farted.

'He's OK! He's OK!' cried Miss Clegg, kissing him on the head. 'Oh I'm so sorry I ever left you.'

Our class cheered.

Gamble turned to me. 'I . . . just . . . needed . . . a friend,' he whispered hoarsely.

I clasped his hands in mine. 'I'm your friend!' I said. And I realised then that, for all his crazy faults and his weird behaviour, Gamble is still my best mate.

But then I saw it. Blood. Oozing out of Gamble's chest.

'Help!' I cried. 'Call an ambulance! He's bleeding to death.'

Panic rippled through the crowd.

'Please don't die!' I begged, tears streaking down my face.

But Gamble opened one eye and looked at me. ''S'not blood,' he said, sitting up, 'it's jam.'

He reached into his pocket and pulled something out. Something round and wrapped in sweaty old tissue paper.

I squinted at it. 'Hang on,' I said. 'Isn't that . . .'

He unwrapped it. And there, on his palm, was a doughnut. Shrivelled and soggy like your fingers after a long bath – but a doughnut nonetheless.

'It's the one you dropped in the bin when we first got here,' he said weakly. 'I came up and crawled into the bin and nicked it for you last night but . . . ' he shifted himself uncomfortably, 'you didn't want it.'

'Oh Darren!' I said and, without thinking, I shoved it into my mouth. OK. It was stale. And there was some green stuff on the outside that may or may not have been mould. And it tasted a bit of leftover food and manky wheelie bins.

But, honestly, it was the best doughnut I've ever tasted in my life.

Good Lass

I was interrupted by a piercing cry from over by the car. Mad Dan was on his knees in front of it again, wailing. The bonnet was completely crushed and the windscreen shattered. Meanwhile, Gusher was being led out of the crumpled mess by the farmer and the vet. Miraculously she seemed completely unharmed by the fall.

The TV camera was now pointing at the cow.

'Amazing scenes here!' exclaimed the presenter. 'Cow and boy back on the ground. Let's ask the vet for an update.'

The microphone was shoved under the vet's face, as he squeezed Gusher's sides. 'Well. No bones broken. The air bag saved her. But I'm a bit concerned. Her tummy's very swollen.'

I gulped. *The chicken nuggets.*

At that moment, Rosie shoulder-barged the vet

out of the way and leapt in front of the camera. ‘OMG!’ she declared, ‘this was like the most totes incredible thing ever. I’m, like, wow. This cannot be happening to me. I mean I was just, like . . . wow!’

‘Thank you,’ said the presenter. He tried to push her out of the way but she fought against him. Behind her, Gusher’s tail lifted up slightly.

Oblivious, Rosie continued. ‘So I’ll be doing a report on my YouTube channel – ’

Rosie didn’t get the chance to finish. Behind her back, Gusher had slowly raised her tail, before unleashing an incredible torrent of green liquid straight at the back of Rosie’s head. Her face frozen in unimaginable horror, Rosie was drenched from head to toe in seconds.

‘Keep the camera rolling!’ cried the presenter. ‘This is great telly!’

‘Good lass,’ said the farmer, patting Gusher on the side. ‘Get it all out.’

Epilogue

So earlier I said that chicken nuggets ruined my life. Well, actually, it wasn't completely true.

You see, they *very nearly* ruined my life. And even though things were catastrophic for a few days, those nasty little beasts didn't beat me in the end. . .

I mean, I've got my best mate back, even if he is a total weirdo. And Vanya is still pals with me, which gives me a 100 per cent increase in friends since before the residential. Excellent result!

When Mum found out about all the trouble that the nuggets had caused, she told me they were way too dangerous and allowed me to start eating doughnuts again, right away.

Miss Clegg came back to school with us and, despite everything, she is still Gamble's teaching assistant. She has never mentioned Mad Dan since.

After getting rid of the chicken-nugget blockage from her backside, Gusher was completely fine. As soon as we returned to school, Gamble started sending her letters. As yet, the cow has not replied.

And as for Rosie? Well, by the time the fire brigade had hosed her down and we'd got back to school, her video (*Cow Toilet Girl)* had already gone viral around the world. She's got the fame she wanted. But perhaps not the way she'd planned it . . .

MARK LOWERY grew up in Preston but now lives near Cambridge with his young family. Some of the time he is a primary school teacher. In the olden days he used to spend his time doing lots of active stuff like running, hiking, snowboarding and swimming but now he prefers staying in and attempting to entertain his children. He plays the guitar badly and speaks appalling Italian but he knows a lot about biscuits. In his mind he is one of the great footballers of his generation, although he is yet to demonstrate this on an actual football pitch. He has an MA in Writing for Children and his first two books were both shortlisted for the Roald Dahl Funny Prize. He is yet to find a cake that he doesn't like.

Find out more at
www.marklowery.co.uk

Thank you for choosing a Piccadilly Press book.

If you would like to know more about our authors, our books or if you'd just like to know what we're up to, you can find us online.

www.piccadillypress.co.uk

You can also find us on:

We hope to see you soon!